I0671001

A STRANGE DISCOVERY

Charles Romyn Dake

1st WORLD
LIBRARY
Literary Society

A Strange Discovery

Charles Romyn Dake

© 1st World Library – Literary Society, 2006
PO Box 2211
Fairfield, IA 52556
www.1stworldlibrary.org
First Edition

LCCN: 2006930766

Softcover ISBN: 1-4218-2175-3
Hardcover ISBN: 1-4218-2075-7
eBook ISBN: 1-4218-2275-X

Purchase *"A Strange Discovery"*
as a traditional bound book at:
www.1stWorldLibrary.org/purchase.asp?ISBN=1-4218-2175-3

1st World Library Literary Society is a nonprofit
organization dedicated to promoting literacy by:

- Creating a free internet library accessible from any
  computer worldwide.
- Hosting writing competitions and offering book
  publishing scholarships.

**Readers interested in supporting literacy
through sponsorship, donations or
membership please contact:
literacy@1stworldlibrary.org
Check us out at: www.1stworldlibrary.ORG
and start downloading free ebooks today.**

A Strange Discovery
contributed by Tim, Ed & Rodney
in support of
1st World Library Literary Society

HOW WE FOUND DIRK PETERS

THE FIRST CHAPTER

It was once my good fortune to assist in a discovery of some importance to lovers of literature, and to searchers after the new and wonderful. As nearly a quarter of a century has since elapsed, and as two others shared in the discovery, it may seem to the reader strange that the general public has been kept in ignorance of an event apparently so full of interest. Yet this silence is quite explicable; for of the three participants none has heretofore written for publication; and of my two associates, one is a quiet, retiring man, the other is erratic and forgetful.

It is also possible that the discovery did not at the time impress either my companions or myself as having that importance and widespread interest which I have at last come to believe it really possesses. In any view of the case, there are reasons, personal to myself, why it was less my duty than that of either of the others to place on record the facts of the discovery. Had either of them, in all these years, in ever so brief a manner, done so, I should have remained forever silent.

The narrative which it is my purpose now to put in written form, I have at various times briefly or in part related to one and another of my intimate friends; but they all mistook my facts for fancies, and good-naturedly complimented me on my story-telling powers - which was certainly not flattering to my qualifications as an historian.

With this explanation, and this extenuation of what some persons may think an inexcusable and almost criminal delay, I shall proceed.

In the year 1877 I was compelled by circumstances to visit the States. At that time, as at the present, my home was near Newcastle-upon-Tyne. My father, then recently deceased, had left, in course of settlement in America, business interests involving a considerable pecuniary investment, of which I hoped a large part might be recovered. My lawyer, for reasons which seemed to me sufficient, advised that the act of settlement should not be delegated; and I decided to leave at once for the United States. Ten days later I reached New York, where I remained for a day or two and then proceeded westward. In St. Louis I met some of the persons interested in my business. There the whole transaction took such form that a final settlement depended wholly upon the agreement between a certain man and myself; but, fortunately for the fate of this narrative, the man was not in St. Louis. He was one of those wealthy so-called "kings" which abound in America - in this case a "coal king." I was told that he possessed a really palatial residence in St. Louis - where he *did not* dwell; and a less pretentious dwelling directly in the coal-fields, where, for the most of his time, he *did* reside. I crossed the Mississippi River into Southern Illinois, and very soon found him. He was a plain, honest business man; we did not split hairs, and within a week I had in my pocket London exchange for something like L20,000, he had in his pocket a transfer of my interest in certain coal-fields and a certain railroad, and we were both satisfied.

And now, having explained how I came to be in surroundings to me so strange, any further mention of business, or of money interests, shall not, in the course of this narrative, again appear.

I had arrived at the town of Bellevue, in Southern Illinois, on a bright June morning, and housed myself in an old-fashioned, four-story brick hotel, the Loomis House, in which the proprietor, a portly, ruddy-faced, trumpet-voiced man, assigned to me an apartment - a spacious corner room, with three windows looking upon the main thoroughfare and two upon a side street, and a smaller room adjoining.

Here, even before the time came when I might have returned to England had I so desired, I acquired quite a home-like feeling. The first two days of my stay, as I had travelled rapidly and was somewhat wearied, I allotted to rest, and left my room for little else than the customary tri-daily visits to the *table d'hote.*

During these first two days I made many observations from my windows, and asked numberless questions of the bell-boy. I learned that a certain old, rambling, two-story building directly across the side street was the hotel mentioned by Dickens in his "American Notes," and in the lower passage-way of which he met the Scotch phrenologist, "Doctor Crocus." The bell-boy whom I have mentioned was the factotum of the Loomis House, being, in an emergency, hack-driver, porter, runner - all by turns, and nothing long at a time. He was a quaint genius, named Arthur; and his position, on the whole, was somewhat more elevated than that of our English "Boots." During these two days I became quite an expert in the invention of immediate personal wants; for, as I continued my studies of local life from the windows of my apartment, I frequently desired information, and would then ring my bell, hoping that Arthur would be the person to respond, as he usually was. He was an extremely profane youth, but profane in a quiet, drawling, matter-of-fact manner. He was frequently semi-intoxicated by noon, and sometimes quite inarticulate by 9 P.M.; but I never saw him with his bodily equilibrium seriously impaired - in plainer words, I never saw him stagger. He openly confessed to a weakness for an occasional glass, but would have repelled with scorn, perhaps with blows, an insinuation attributing to him excess in that direction. True, he referred to times in his life when he had been "caught" - meaning that the circumstances were on those occasions such as to preclude any successful denial of intoxication; but these occasions, it was implied, dated back to the period of his giddy youth.

With little to occupy my mind (I had the St. Louis dailies, one of which was the best newspaper - excepting, of course, our *Times* - that I have ever read; but my trunks did not arrive until a day or two later, and I was without my favorite books), I became really interested in studying the persons whom I saw passing and repassing the hotel, or stopping to converse on the opposite street-corners; and after forming surmises concerning those of them who most interested me, I would ask Arthur who they were, and then compare with my own opinions the truth as furnished by him.

There was a quiet, well-dressed young man, who three or four times each day passed along the side street. Regarding him, I had formed and altered my opinion several times; but I finally determined that he was a clergyman in recent orders and just come to town. When I asked Arthur whether I was correct in my surmise, he answered:

"Wrong again - that is, on the fellow's business" - I had not before made an erroneous surmise; but on the contrary, had shown great penetration in determining, at a single glance for each of them, two lawyers and a banker - "Yes, sir, wrong again; and right again, too. His name's Doctor Bainbridge, and he's fool enough to come here with the town just alive with other sawbones. He's some kind of a 'pathy doctor, come here to learn us how to get well on sugar and wind - or pretty near that bad. He don't give no medicine worth mentionin', he keeps his hoss so fat he can't trot, and he ain't got no wife to mend his clothes. They say he's gettin' along, though; and old farmer Vagary's boy that had 'em, told me he was good on fits - but I don't believe *that*, for the boy had the worst fit in his life after he told me. The doctor said - so they tell - as that was jest what he expected, and that he was glad the fit came so hard, for it show'd the medicine was workin'."

My attention was particularly attracted to a man who daily, in fact almost hourly, stood at an opposite corner, and who frequently arrived, or drove away, in a buggy drawn by two rather small, black, spirited horses. He was a tall, lithe, dark-complexioned man, with black eyes, rather long black hair, and a full beard; extremely restless, and constantly moving back and forth. He addressed many passers-by, a fair proportion of whom stopped to exchange a word with him. In the latter instance, however, the exchange was scarcely equitable, as he did the talking, and his remarks, judging by his gestures of head and hand, were generally emphatic.

One of the apparently favorite positions which he assumed was to throw an arm around the corner gas-post, and swing his body back and forth, occasionally, when alone, taking a swing entirely around the post. Another favorite position was to stand with his fists each boring into the hollow of his back over the corresponding hip, with his chest and shoulders thrown well back, and his head erect, looking steadily off into the distance. With regard to this man's station in life, I took little credit to myself for a correct guess; for, in addition to other aids to correct guessing, the store-room on that corner was occupied by an apothecary. When I asked Arthur whether the man was not a physician, "Yes, sir," he replied; "physician, surgeon, and obstetrician; George F. Castleton, A.M., M.D. *He* ought to get a dry-goods box and a torch-light, and sell 'Hindoo Bitters' in the Public-square. If you jest want to die quick, you know where to go to get it. That fellow salivated me till my teeth can't keep quiet. Oh, he knows it all! Medicine ain't enough to fill his intellecty. *He* runs the Government and declares war to suit himself. 'Moves around a great deal,' you say? Well, I believe you; but when you see his idees move around you'll quit sighing about his body. Why, sir, that man in a campaign changes his politics every day; nobody ever yet caught up with his religion; and besides, he's a prophet. You jest get back home without touchin' *him*, if you love me, now, please do."

All of this was said in a quiet, instructive tone, without much show of feeling even when the teeth were mentioned, and only such emphasis as has been indicated by my italics. Arthur's advice for me to get home without "touching" the doctor, I had no intention of following. My curiosity regarding the man was aroused, and I had determined, if possible, to know him. So far as one could be influenced from a third-story window, I was favorably impressed with him. I judged him to be superlatively erratic, but without an atom of real evil in his being. I had observed from my window an incident that gave me a glance into the man's heart. A poor, dilapidated, distressed negro, evidently seeking help, had come running up to him as he stood near his buggy, at the corner; and the manner in which he pushed the negro into the buggy, himself followed, and then started off at a break-neck speed, left no doubt in my mind that the doctor had a heart as large as the whole world. Once or twice during the long, warm afternoons, his words came to me through the open windows. I was aware that his almost preternaturally bright, quick eyes flashed a glance or two at me as I once or twice stepped rather close to an open window looking out over the lower roof-tops beyond; and I felt that he had given me a niche in his mind, as I had him in mine. I wondered if he had formed mental estimates of my status, and if so whether he had attempted to corroborate them as did I mine, through Arthur. Once I heard him say to a small, craven-looking man, apparently feeble in mind and in body, with red, contracted, watering eyes, "Yes, sir, if I had been Sam Tilden, the blood in these streets would have touched your stirrups" - the little man had no stirrups - "This country is trembling over an abyss deeper'n the infernal regions. Ha, ha! What a ghastly burlesque on human freedom! Now, hark you, Pickles" - the small man was not only listening, but, I could imagine, trembling. He would now and then look furtively around, as if fearing that somebody else might hear the doctor, and that war would begin - "listen to me: 'Hell has no fury like a nation scorned.'" Here Doctor Castleton shot a glance at the little man, to see whether or not so fine a stroke was appreciated, and whether his quotation was or was not passing as original. "I repeat, 'Hell has no fury like a nation scorned' - *Nation*, you hear, Pickles - *nation*, not woman. There is just one thing to save this crumbling Republic; give us more paper money - greenbacks on greenbacks, mountain high. Let the Government rent by the month or lease by the year every printing-press in the country - let the machinery sweetly hum as the sheets of treasury-notes fall in cascades to the floor, to be cut apart, packed in bundles, and sent to any citizen who wants them on his own unendorsed note - *un*endorsed, Pickles, and at two per cent.! Ever study logic, Pickles? No! Well, no matter; my brain's full enough of the stuff for both of us. If the American citizen is honest - which I opine that he is - the scheme will work like a charm; if he is *dis*honest - which God forbid, and let no man assert - then let the country sink - and the sooner the better. I pity the imbecile that can't see this point. The people - and *is* this country for the *people*, or is it not? — follow me, Pickles: the people obtain plenty of money, the stores get it, the factories and importers get it, and commerce hums." Here the doctor was for a moment diverted by some objective impression; and without a word of excuse to the little man, he swung himself into his buggy, which stood waiting, and drove rapidly away; whilst the diminutive man, after a moment of weak indecision, shuffled off down the street. I later learned that these talks of Doctor Castleton's were, as regards the element of verity, thrown off as writers of fiction throw off fancies. Sometimes he defended opinions that were in fierce conflict with the ideas of his auditors; but he generally talked to please them, frequently assuming as his own, and in exaggerated form, the hobbies, notions, or desires of his auditors. In the incident just recorded, the doctor probably had not, as a matter of fact, been stating his real opinions, though for the moment he may have imagined that he was an uncompromising "Paper-money man" or "Greenbacker," as a member of one of the minor political parties of the day was termed: the little man was poor, and Doctor Castleton had simply been drawing for him a picture of delights - at least, so I conjectured. This propensity of the doctor sometimes led to startling surprises and results, and, once at least, to a discovery of weighty consequence - as we shall soon perceive.

It was novelty for me, and under the circumstances often quite refreshing, to witness the manner in which Americans treated the mighty subjects of life, and spoke of the great and powerful persons of the earth. It was an abundant source of entertainment for me to ask almost anybody with whom I happened to be conversing, for his opinion on some great subject or of some noted personage; for the reply was always to me unique, sometimes very amusing, and not infrequently instructive. On the way for the second time from our evening meal to my room, I stopped for a moment in the "Gentlemen's sitting-room," where I in part overheard a conversation between an elderly and a middle-aged man. I afterward learned that the younger man was a lawyer, by name Lill; that he was well known throughout the State, a man of cultivation, very conventional in his private life, but an unequivocal dissenter on almost every great social question; a man of high honor, and unquestionable personal habits, for whom exalted public office had often waited if only he could have modified his expressed opinions to less inharmony with those of men who held the reins of power. It seemed that these two men had not met for a year or more; and as I entered the room they were comparing experiences, in a leisurely, confidential, sympathetic way. As I came within hearing, the lawyer had just started in afresh, after a laugh and a pause. Settling-down his features, and assuming a more-news-to-be-told manner, with a pinch of fine-cut tobacco between finger and thumb ready to go into his mouth, and leaning slightly forward to keep the tobacco-dust from his shirt-front, he said, "Well, David, I read the Bible through again last winter, and I must continue to think it a very immoral book. Its teaching is really bad. Why, sir, what would you think of such d - -d outrageous teaching if anybody were at this time to promulgate it with an implication of any practical relation to present events?" And so he continued, somewhat, though not greatly, to the horror of his companion, who seemed to be a Christian - at least by descent. On another day, after the mid-day meal, as I again entered this room, I observed a new-comer in conversation with what I took to be a small delegation of Bellevue business men. I was afterward presented to this new arrival, when I learned that his name was Rowell - General Rowell; a name which I thought I had seen in the newspapers at home. He was a large man of prepossessing appearance, and gave me the impression of considerable mental force and activity. I heard him say to his visitors - the words apparently closing a conference: "Yes, gentlemen, if I come to Bellevue, and we build a nail mill in your city, I ask only five years time in which to make our mill the largest nail-works in the world." For a moment, as I heard this remark, it passed through my mind that I was in the presence of an excellent example of an amusing type of American life; but the momentary thought was erroneous. This man was one of a type of American - well, of American promoters, I will say - the business plans of whom, though mammoth and audacious, rarely fail - the genuine article of which the Colonel Sellerses are but pitiful imitators. In this instance, the promise was fulfilled, with a year or two to spare. The right to express personal opinion was looked upon as one of the fruits of 76, and the value of such opinion seemed to be measured almost wholly on its merits - even to a laughable extent. For instance, this lawyer, or Doctor Castleton, or any other American whom I met, whatever he might privately have thought on the subject, would not for a moment have claimed that his opinion was innately superior to that of, for instance, the factotum, Arthur. A man seemed to have, also, an inalienable right to be a snob; but I saw in America only one man who utilized that privilege. I heard an Ex-Governor of the State express himself on this subject by the concise remark: "We have no law *here* against a man making a d - d fool of himself." It's "Abe" for the President of the Republic, "Dick" for the Governor of the State, and so on, all the way through. But no one should imagine that admiration as well as respect for the truly great of the land is less than it is where a man with four names and two inherited titles receives greater homage than does one with only three names and one title. Customs differ in different lands - a trite remark; but it is about all that can be said on the subject: after all, human feeling is not extremely different in different lands, when we once get back of mere form.

I might illustrate a part of my statement by relating an incident which occurred on my third day in the hotel, and just prior to my emergence from seclusion into the midst of the busy little city. I was in my sitting-room, and Arthur had brought in a pitcher of ice-water, placing it on a table. Then he paused and looked toward me, as if expecting the usual question on some subject connected with my surroundings. But at the time I had nothing to ask. After a moment of quiet, Arthur spoke:

"Did you see the Prince lately?" he inquired. I had by this time grown so accustomed to Arthur's mode of thought and lingual expression, that even this question did not greatly surprise me. I supposed that the query was made on the first suggestion of an alert mind desirous of starting a little agreeable conversation, and wishing to be sociable with a "two-room" guest. He immediately continued:

"I hope he's well. I met him, you know, when he was over here, sev'ral years ago, gettin' idees for his kingdom."

I began to feel amused. Arthur was not a liar, and anything but a bore: he struck me as being truthful on all subjects except that of his bibulous weakness - a subject on which he was, perhaps naturally, not able to form accurate notions.

"Where did you meet His Highness, Arthur?" I asked.

"Oh, in Pittsburg, Pennsylvania. I was only eight then. They wouldn't let boys in the hotel to see him, and there was so many big-wigs around the young man, I couldn't get to see him at first. But after a while they all got out in front of the hotel, to get into their carriages. They had to wait a few minutes, but I couldn't get in front to see him. The hotel hall was empty by that time, and everybody was looking at the Prince; so I hurried through the barber-shop into the side hall; slipped along into the main hall, to the main entrance. I was not more than ten or twelve feet from the Prince, but I was at the back of the crowd; so I jest got down on all-fours, and crawled in between their legs. I got clear up to the Prince, but

Charles Romyn Dake

a big man stood on each side of him, right close up. For a minute I thought I was worse off than ever. Then I noticed that the Prince had his legs a little separate - his knees were maybe six inches apart, with one leg standin' ahead of the other. I was a little fellow, even for eight; and I saw my chance. I ran my head in between his knees and twisted my body and neck so as to look right up into his face, as he looked down to see what rubbed against him. He looked kind of funny when he saw my face down there, but not a bit mad; and he could easy have hurt me, but he didn't. I drew back my head so quick that nobody else saw me. I often wonder if the Prince remembers me; and I wish you'd ask him when you go home. Since I grew up, I've often felt ashamed to think I did it. If you think of it, and it ain't too much trouble, please tell him that we know better in the United States than to do such things, but that I was little then, and I must have been ignorant of ettiket, my father bein' dead, and I havin' to stay out of school to help make money. If you will, say I hope there's no feelin ; and when you think of it, drop me a line, please."

THE SECOND CHAPTER

A week had elapsed since my arrival in Bellevue. I had been introduced to Doctor Castleton, and had exchanged a few words with him. I had also listened to several of his street-corner talks, and my interest in him from day to day had increased. This interest must have been reciprocal, for he seemed to look for my coming; but then, in whom was he not interested? I liked him for his real goodness, was entertained by his erratic ways, and admired his intellectual brightness. Never before had I come in contact with a mind at once so spontaneous and so versatile. It was perhaps his most striking peculiarity, that he seemed always to be looking for something startling to occur; and in a dearth of the new and sensational from without, he produced excitement for the community from within. The weather, for instance, was growing warmer, and the summer was apparently to be a sultry one: hence, before the season was ended we were to look for the most sweeping epidemics of disease; a comet had been sighted by one of our comet-hunters, and we were all to say later whether or not it would have been better if we'd never been born, and so on, and so on. His mind teemed with a prescience of the plans and plots of statesmen, of bureaucrats, and of "plutocrats": Germany was going to overshadow Europe, and "grind all beneath it like a glacier"; "France was about to strike back at Prussia, and the blow would be felt in the trembling of the earth from Pole to Pole." Yet this, I thought, was to the man himself all fiction - the froth on the limpid and sparkling depths beneath - the overflow of a bright, undisciplined mind amid the stagnation of a country town. This strange man

Charles Romyn Dake

would not intentionally have brought actual injury upon ever an enemy - if he ever had a real enemy; he was at heart, and generally in practice, as kind as a gentle woman. But he seemed unable to exist without mental super-activity; and the sympathy of his fellows in his mental gyrations was to him a constant necessity. Few of the persons whom he habitually met and who had leisure were able to discuss with him the books he read, and not many of them cared even to hear him talk of his fresh literary accessions. He had, long ago, and many times, described for the benefit of the habitues of the corners, the career of Alexander and of Napoleon, explaining what they had done, and how they had done it, and *why*; with instances in which the execution of their plans had met with failure, the reasons for that failure, and the methods by which, if *he* had been them, success might easily have been attained. An ancient-looking apothecary, with an old "Rebel bushwhacker ' and a painter out of work who "loafed" of evenings in, or in front of, the corner apothecary shop, had stood gap-mouthed at these recitations until the mine of wonders had been to the last grain exhausted. Still, excitement must be procured for them. The doctor could better have dispensed for a day with food for the body, than to have foregone excitement for the mind; and if a majority of his auditors were also to be gratified, the subject-matter must be strong and novel, must be boldly produced, and, by preference, should be of local interest. As the doctor himself delighted in surprises of a terrifying or horrifying nature, it was unlikely that his inventions in that direction would be characterized by tameness. He would not, when hard pressed on a dull day, allow a fastidious care of even his own reputation to impede the development of one of his surprises. If the town of Bellevue was to stagnate mentally, it would not be the fault of George F. Castleton, A.M., M.D.

It was on the eighth day of my stay in Bellevue, that, on starting forth from the hotel one morning, I saw Doctor Castleton standing before the Loomis House, in one of his favorite attitudes - that is, with his head and shoulders thrown back and his hands upon his hips - looking intently at a young man who stood speaking with an aged farmer across the way, near the street curbing - a harmless-looking youth, with dark blue eyes, and straight, very dark hair - in fact, the clerical-looking young man whom I had seen from my windows. Something in the man's make-up - perhaps something in his attire - suggested the stranger in town. Doctor Castleton's large black eyes flashed irefully, and he was evidently gratified at my approach. A complete stranger in my place might have thought his arrival opportune, and have looked upon himself as a diverting instrument in higher hands employed to prevent bloodshed. As I stopped by the doctor's side, he said, with ill-suppressed agitation.

"That d - d villain over there has got to leave town. He calls himself a doctor, but I have set in motion the wheels of the law of this great State of Illinois, and I'll expose the infernal rascal." Then, with a dark, knowing look at me, he hissed (though none of his preceding words had been audible across the street), "An 'Irregular,' sir - cursed sugar-and-water quack - a figure 9 with the tail rubbed off. Why, sir" (in a more conversational but still emphatic tone), "*I* have given sixty grains of calomel at a dose, and I have given a tenth of a grain of calomel at a dose; I would give a man a hundred grains of quinine, and I have done it; I have" (and here he took from his pocket a small round lozenge or button of bone) " - I have bored into the brains of man - into the Corinthian Capital of Mortality, so to speak. When that man" (pointing with his right forefinger to the circle of bone in his left palm) "was kicked in the head by his mule, three of my colleagues were on the scene before me - standing around like old women, doing nothing. *I* have elaborate instruments, sir - I don't read any more books - the world's literature is here" (tapping his forehead). "I've thought too much to care for other men's ideas. Like old women, I was saying, sir. 'Give me a poker,' I yelled - ' give me anything.' I sent for my trephine. Great God, how the blood flew, and the bone creaked! I raised the depressed bone. The man lives. I've done everything, in my life. And now a cursed quack comes to town - . Where's his wife? I say - where's his suffering children? - Don't tell me, anybody, that the man's not married, and run away from his

Charles Romyn Dake

suffering wife. Take his trail; glide like the wily savage back over his course, and mark me, sir, you'll trace the pathway of a besom of destruction: weeping mothers, broken-hearted fathers, daughters bowed in the dust. What's he here for? Why didn't he stay where he was? But I'll drive him out of town - you will see - bag and baggage: the wires are set - the avalanche approaches - he is doomed."

Two days later, at the same spot, I came upon Doctor Castleton in conversation with the harmless-looking young man, to whom the doctor formally presented me. The name of the young man, as stated by Castleton, and as I already knew, was "Doctor Bainbridge." We exchanged a few words, he extended to me an invitation to call upon him, and he accepted an urgent request from me to visit me at the hotel. As my stay in America would probably last but a few days longer, I proposed that the evening of that same day be selected as the time for his visit, and to this proposal he readily assented. Then, with a quiet smile, he bowed and left us. As he walked away Doctor Castleton remarked,

"That young man is a genius, sir. Belongs to the Corinthian Capital of Mortality. Trust me, sir, he's the coming man in this town. He will be a power here, in the years to come. I read a man, sir, as you would read a book."

I then invited Doctor Castleton to come to my rooms that evening, even if he could spare no more than a few moments: and he promised to come, "Though," he said, "I may not be able more than to run in, and run out again." Bainbridge, the new Bellevue candidate for medical practice, could devote his hours as he should elect; but Castleton, "for twenty years the guardian of the lives of thousands," must abstract, as best he might, a few minutes from the onerous duties entailed by the exacting wishes of his many invalid patrons.

Later in the day, I made arrangements for a little luncheon to be served that evening in my rooms. There was something about this Bainbridge that impelled me to know him better. I had already made up my mind that I should like him: his were those clear blue eyes that calmly seemed to understand the world around - truth-loving eyes. He had to my mind the appearance of a person with large capacity for physical pleasure, yet that of one who possessed complete control over every like and dislike of his being. I at first took him to be extremely reticent; but later I learned, that, when the proper chord of sympathy was touched, he responded in perfect torrents of spoken confidence. So I that evening sat in the larger of my rooms - my "sitting-room" - in momentary expectation of the arrival of one or both of my invited guests.

Charles Romyn Dake

THE THIRD CHAPTER

The hour was about eight. I had written a letter or two after our six o'clock supper, and was now idle. By my side, in the centre of the room, stood a table on which lay several periodicals - monthly and weekly, English and American - a newspaper or two, and a few books. A rap came at my door, and on opening it I found Doctor Bainbridge standing in the hallway. He wore a black "Prince Albert" coat, a high silk hat, and, the evening having blown-up chilly, a summer overcoat. I received him perhaps a little more warmly than was in the best of taste, considering that we had not before exchanged more than a dozen words. But I had, as I have said, frequently seen him from my window; he was almost as much of a stranger in the town as was I, and I received him cordially because my feelings were really cordial. I assisted him to remove his coat, and in other ways did all in my power to make him comfortable. He was of slightly more than medium height, of rather delicate build, with a fair, almost colorless complexion. His movements, his language, his attire, indicated the gentleman - this I should have conceded him in my club at home, or in my own drawing-room, quite as readily as here, alone, in an obscure hotel in the State of Illinois. As we sat conversing, I was much surprised to find in him a considerable degree of culture. He seemed to possess that particular air which we are accustomed to think, and generally with reason, is not to be found apart from a familiarity with metropolitan life on its highest plane. I did not on that evening, nor did I later, think him thoroughly schooled, except in his profession. He was, however, fairly well educated, and his opinions seemed to me from my own stand-point to be sound. I had observed, in a history of the county just from the press, which lay on a table in the office of the hotel, that in 1869 he had been graduated from an educational institution somewhere in Pennsylvania; and, in 1873, from the Medical Department of Columbia University. Later, I learned from himself, that, from the age of seven to the age of eleven, he had been instructed at home by a sister who was some nine or ten years his senior.

I seated him with the large centre-table between us, and immediately opened the conversation on some topic of local interest. It is probable that of the many persons whom I know and continue to like, that I liked nine out of ten of them from our first meeting. Doctor Bainbridge had not been long in my presence before I knew that my first impressions of him were not deceptive; and I felt that his impression of myself was certainly not unfavorable.

It appeared to me as we talked through the evening, that he had read about all that I had read, and much besides. He talked of English and French history with minute familiarity. Not only had he read English, French, and German literature, with such Spanish, Russian, and Italian works as had been translated into English; but he shamed me with the thoroughness of his knowledge of Scott, Dickens, Bulwer, Thackeray, and others of our best writers of fiction. Goethe he particularly admired. Of Cervantes he thought with the rest of us: He had read "Don Quixote," for the first time, when he was eighteen, and during a severe illness accompanied with intense melancholia; and he had laughed himself out of bed, and out of his melancholy. "Don Quixote" was, he said, the only book which he had ever read in solitude - that is, read to himself - which had compelled him to laugh aloud. Works of science, particularly scientific works in the domain of physics, he delighted in. His imagination was of a most charming character. It was at that time in my life almost a passion with me to analyze human nature - to theorize over the motives and the results of human action; over the probable causes of known or assumed effects, and the reverse - in short, I thought myself a philosopher. I have never met another person whom it so much interested me to study as it did this young American. But after ample opportunity to know him, even now as I sit writing more than twenty years later, and I think of the pleasure of that temporary friendship in far-away Illinois, I am puzzled about many things concerning Doctor Bainbridge. He certainly possessed a scientific mind. He himself said that he had no very great love for written poetry: had he a poetic mind? He loved the beautiful in life: he loved symmetry in form, he loved harmony in color, he loved good music. And yet, though he had read the English-writing poets, he seemed to care less for their work than for anything else in literature. The thought of this inconsistency has perplexed me whenever I have thought of it through all these years. As I have intimated, he was charmed by the beautiful, and by every known expression of beauty; but for the strictly metrical in language-expression, he evinced almost a distaste. I have often thought that he had, through some peculiar circumstance in his earlier life, acquired a suggestive dislike to the very form of verse. To this peculiarity there was, however, exception, to which I am about to allude.

By the time we had smoked out a cigar apiece, we were exchanging views and comments on such writers, English and American, as came to mind. One of the books that lay on my table was a copy of Byron; though most of the others were the works of American authors - Hawthorne, Irving, Longfellow, Poe, and one or two others. He had picked up my Byron, and glancing at it had remarked that if all the poets were like Byron he would devote more time than he did to the reading of verse. I recall a remark that, with Byron's personality in mind, he made as he returned the book to the table. "Poor fellow!" he said. "But what are we to expect of a man who had a volcano for a mother, and an iceberg for a wife? A woman's character is largely formed by the quality of men that enter into her life; a man's, even more so by the quality of women that enter into his. I wonder if Byron ever intimately knew a true woman? - a woman at once intellectually and morally normal, in a good wholesome way - a woman with a good brain and a warm heart? No man, in my opinion, is a really good man save through the influence of good women."

It is impossible for me to recall much of what he said of the American authors of whom we talked, with the exception of Poe; and there are reasons why I should clearly remember in substance, and almost in words, everything that was said of him. Of all writers, with one exception, Poe interests me the most; and I judge that in interest, both as a personality and as a literary artist, Doctor Bainbridge placed Edgar Allan Poe first and uppermost among those who have left to the world a legacy of English verse or prose. And this feeling was, I truly believe, in no measure influenced by Poe's nationality. If Bainbridge possessed any narrow national prejudices I never learned of them.

He spoke rapturously of Poe as a poet - "The Raven," as a matter of course, receiving high praise: Of that unique and really grand poem, he said that he thought it the best in the English language.

It was at this point in our conversation that he told me he rarely read verse; that he had, with certain exceptions, never done so with much pleasure, but that in some way he had managed to read nearly all the noted poetry published in our language. Still, he said, there were poems which absorbed and almost fascinated him. Of the English poets of the present century, Byron alone had written enough poetry to prove himself a poet; and he explained that in his opinion the writing of an occasional or chance poem, though the poem were true poetry, did not make of the author a poet. Then he mentioned a poem which for more than a century has been by the critical world accepted as of the highest order of true poetry. Gradually warming to the subject, he said:

"A poem like this is not to my mind poetry. Byron wrote true poetry, and sufficient of it in his short life to prove himself ten times over a poet. To compare this poem with Byron's poetry - say with parts of 'Childe Harold,' or 'The Prisoner of Chillon,' or with some of his shorter poems - would be like comparing the most perfect mechanical device with a graceful animal - say the mechanical imitation of a tiger or a gazelle with the living original; the first a wonderfully moving piece of machinery, illustrating the limit of human constructive power; perfectly under control, the movements smooth, unvarying, rhythmical, charming, excelling in agility and power its living prototype - but still, scientific - to the discerning eye, artful. The other, something more than rhythmical, more than smooth, beyond the control of human agency, beyond the power of man to analyze as to synthetize - more than science can explain, more than even art dare claim. The one explicable, the other inexplicable; the one from the hand of patient skill - of talent; the other a result of force mysterious, divine. The lions of Alexius Comnenus, it is said, could roar louder than the lions of the desert."

"But what of Poe, and 'The Raven?'" I asked.

"The surprising thing about 'The Raven' is," he said, "and I assert only what I believe to be from internal evidence demonstrable - first, that the poem arose out of a true poetic impulse of the soul; and, second, that it discloses the very highest art possible to a writer. Now I truly believe that the first writing of 'The Raven' - and, too, the stanzas were probably not first written in their present published order - conveyed Poe's poetic sense just as completely as the published poem now does. But this was not sufficient for Edgar Allan Poe - for the scientific man, the artful man, the poetic genius with a genius for concentrated mental toil in the effort to attain literary perfection. This makes 'The Raven' a curiosity in true poetic expression.'

"Then you believe," I said, "that both the state of feeling from which true poetry arises, and the particular words by which the feeling is conveyed, are inspired."

"I do. But Poe was able actually to improve the language of inspiration, whilst transmitting uninjured the poetic conception. Those stanzas in Grey's 'Elegy' which convey from him to us the psychic wave of poetic impulse, may have been hundreds of times altered in their wording, through seven years of tentative effort; and it is possible that he succeeded in retaining the original feeling - the poem is certainly artistic. But the feeling conveyed by Grey is commonplace enough, anyway; whilst that transmitted by Poe is wholly unique, and intensely absorbing - indeed, a startling revelation. I have always felt that Byron, Milton, Shakespeare, found within their souls their poetry, and that the linguistic expression of it came to them as naturally as did the feeling."

"Such minds," I said, "will always be a mystery to common mortals."

"I take it," replied Bainbridge, "that waves and wavelets of poetic feeling are common enough among men - quite as common as mental pictures of beautiful material images; but the rarity is in the word-conception, which I hold must as a rule be spontaneous if it is to convey unblemished the original feeling. The musical genius is able to convey his psychic impression in harmonious sounds; the true poet, in words. To the rest of us the process is, as you say, a mystery - we call it inspiration.

"Take an isolated poem, such as under, say patriotic feeling, springs from the mind of one who never again writes poetry; does this not help to prove my theory that all true poetry is a result of inspiration - is in its inception and in its word-expression quite extraneous to its apparent author?

"To both my intellect and my feeling, 'The Raven' stands a beautiful masterpiece, which, because it is both the product of a strange psychic state and the work of intellect will probably be the last poem, of those now extant, to be admired by the human race when intellectual development and growth shall finally have driven from the lives and the minds of men all romance, all sentiment, all poetry, leaving to the race only intellect and will."

Charles Romyn Dake

After some further talk, and in reply to a statement of my own Bainbridge said,

"Of course I can speak only for myself; and for me there is music in the poetry of Byron and of Poe, and there is the psychic effect of color. The rhythm in certain of their poems, with the arrangement of word-sound, produces the saddest music possible, I think, to the soul of man - a prevailing monotone so measured as to result in an effect decidedly strange and quite indescribable. But the real peculiarity of their poetry - and in this Poe excels Byron - is a psychic effect the same as that which remains after viewing certain pictures in black and white, the shade gradations of which are so artistic as to create an illusion of color - sombre, highly shaded, yet color. This color effect of Poe's poetry I have felt very slightly, if at all, immediately on a first reading, as I feel the music of his verse - a rereading, or the lapse of time, being required for its full development. I have not read a line of Poe in the last two or three years, and at the present moment I feel *Ulalume* as I would some weird scene or picture viewed long ago."

I asked him what particular color effects Poe's poetry produced in his mind, and he replied,

"The impression of red I do not at all retain. That of black, more or less intense, is predominant; but the color effects of almost any variegated landscape - red being excluded, and the scene having been viewed by moonlight, or in the dusk of evening, or possibly on a densely clouded day - is at this moment alive within me. And yet, with a single exception, I have never received from musical or other sounds a psychic color effect - the exception being that certain tones of a violin leave the same mental impression as does the sight of purple. As I am not acquainted with the technical language of either painter or musician, I can attempt to describe these effects only in common language. I speak for myself only, and am anything but dogmatic on the subject of poetry. The symbolism of Poe's verse we must solve, each for himself. To me, for myself, the solution seems not difficult - and so no doubt says another;

but on comparison these solutions would no doubt be very different."

But highly as Bainbridge estimated Poe's verse, he placed Poe even higher among writers of prose fiction than among poets. As I have said, I am myself an admirer of Poe. His prose I have always thought the work of a true genius - something, as Doctor Bainbridge said, "more than art, aided by the most perfect art." But when we came to speak of his prose writings, Bainbridge was able to express in language all that I had felt of Poe, and to disclose and explain components of his genius that I had never before fully recognized.

I then asked Bainbridge what it was in Poe's prose that he so much admired.

"Poe's strong element of power as a writer of short stories," said Bainbridge, "is, I think, his scientific imagination - the same capacity, strange as the statement may appear, that, when directed into another channel, makes a great physicist. It strikes me as inaccurate to say that Newton discovered the law of gravitation. Newton imagined the fact of a law of physical gravitation; and then he proceeded to prove *the* law of gravitation, accomplishing the discovery by means of a second attribute of genius - viz., tireless mental energy - the possession of a talent for rigorous mental application and severe nervous strain. In the sense that Columbus discovered America - in that sense, Newton discovered the law of gravitation: Columbus imagined an America, and then proceeded to make a physical demonstration of his belief by discovering the Bahamas. The same faculty - scientific imagination - in Poe gave us 'A Descent into the Maelstrom, The Murders in the Rue Morgue,' and other of his tales. And not alone in physics, but in metaphysics, did his imagination open up to him just conceptions; so that in the field of both healthy and morbid mental action his 'intuitive' knowledge was unerring. 'The Fall of the House of Usher' is so true to the real in conception, and so consummate in portrayal, that the more one knows about the mind, the more he inclines to wonder whether these compositions might not have been aided by actual personal experience. Yet these delineations are purely imaginative. Take 'The Imp of the Perverse, The Tell-Tale Heart,' and similar of his stories, not all of which could in reason have come within the experience of one man, and which are undoubtedly grounded upon intuitive suggestion."

I asked him which of Poe's tales he thought the best.

"That would indeed be difficult to determine," he replied. "If the criterion is to be my own intellectual enjoyment, I should mention one; if my feelings, then another. It is possible that I might select one in which my intellectual enjoyment, and my feelings pure and simple, were about equally engaged. We shall probably agree that the most important object of fiction is to produce in the reader a state of feeling, just as musical composition is intended to produce a state of feeling - the short story being comparable with a brief musical production intended to produce a single variety of emotion; the novel, to the music of an opera with its many parts, intended each to excite a particular state of feeling. Naturally prose fiction may, and almost necessarily does, have other objects. Now the reading of 'The Fall of the House of Usher' produces a certain state of emotion, and that wholly apart from any appeal to intellect; no endeavor to do more than produce that state of feeling is made, nothing more than that is effected, and that much is attained in a manner which no pen that has traced short-story fiction, save that of Poe, has ever accomplished. Hence, if the production of feeling - an appeal to the purely moral side of the triangle of mind - be the paramount essential in fiction, 'The Fall of the House of Usher' is the best short story in the English language."

Here Doctor Bainbridge rose from his chair, and taking a turn or two across the floor, continued, in tones indicating vexation,

"Why has not somebody with a ray of the imagination necessary to a comprehension of Poe's genius given us at least a decent sketch of his brief life! Was Poe in a state of mental aberration when he made Griswold his literary executor? Is the world forever to hear of him only from those who see the dark side of his life and know nothing of his life's work? - from those who look at his life and his life's work through the smoked glass of their dull provincial minds? Let us hope for an assay of what is left to us of Poe - an assay which, not wholly ignoring the little dross, will still lose no grain of the pure, virgin gold, and give to the world something approaching what is due to the genius himself, and what, with such a subject, is due to the world."

"Let me alter my question - or, I should say, ask a different one," I said, when he had again seated himself: "Which of Poe's stories most interested you? From which did you receive the most satisfaction?"

"I have been more occupied and interested by 'The Narrative of A. Gordon Pym' than by any two or three of his other stories."

I expressed surprise at this avowal; and my comments on what appeared to me to show a peculiar taste implied a desire for explanation. He continued:

"Although 'The Narrative of A. Gordon Pym' has served as a suggestion, or even a pattern, for some of our best recent stories of adventure, and although it has many points of excellence in itself, it is not the story alone, but the opportunity which the story affords of an analysis of Poe's mind, that creates the greater interest for me. I have always been puzzled to find a reasonably adequate cause for the incomplete state of that narrative. The supposition that Poe had not at his disposal, at the moment he required it, the necessary time for its completion is an hypothesis which I only mention to dispose of. At its close he wrote and added to the narrative a 'Note' of nearly a thousand words; and in the time required for the penning of that addition, he could have brought the story to - perhaps an abrupt, but still, an artistic close. No. Then did Poe not complete 'The Narrative of A. Gordon Pym' because his imagination failed him - failed to supply material of such a quality as his refined and faultless taste demanded? If so, then why did he begin it? Why write more than sixty thousand words in his usual careful and precise style, on a subject to him little known, in to him a new field of literary effort? He could in the time required to write 'The Narrative of A. Gordon Pym' have written from five to ten short stories along familiar lines. No: none of these hypotheses explains the unfinished state of that narrative. My explanation is that the story has a foundation in fact, and that Poe himself never learned more than a foundation for the portion which he wrote. Its leading character next to Pym is one Dirk Peters, a sailor, mutineer, etc. It is my theory that Pym and Peters existed in fact, but that Poe never met either of them, though he did meet sailors who had known Dirk Peters, and that he heard from them the first part of the story, in the form in which it grew to be repeated by seafaring men along the New England coast in the '30s and '40s. Having heard what he supposed to be sufficient, with the aid of his own imagination, to make an interesting story for publication, Poe began and continued to write. Then, as he progressed, he found that his imagination was embarrassed - frustrated by the known facts already employed - whilst it was not assisted by new facts which he was positive existed, but which he could not procure. As he attempted to close the narrative, the cold, written page was a very different thing from what he had conceived it would be as he sat in the tap-room of some New England old 'Sailor's Home,' with a couple of glasses of Burton ale on the table, listening through the drowsy afternoon to the fact and fiction of some old 'tar,' as the two looked across the white-sanded floor at the old moss-grown dock without, and listened to the salt wavelets splashing against its rotting timbers, and watched the far-distant sails on the outer sea. It is not very difficult to picture to one's self Poe searching among these sailors' lodging-houses for Dirk Peters; nor is it unreasonable to assume that he did so search for him. If Dirk Peters was twenty-seven years old in 1827, when the mutiny occurred, he was only forty-nine at the time of Poe's death - in fact, would be only seventy-seven if now alive. Poe says in his 'Note,' that 'Peters, from whom some information might be expected, is still alive, and a resident of Illinois, but cannot be met with at present. He may hereafter be found, and will, no doubt, afford material for a conclusion of Mr. Pym's account.' I have no doubt that Poe eventually learned exactly where Peters resided; but no matter how much Poe may have desired to meet with Peters, he could not have done so. In the '40s it was a long, tedious, expensive journey from New York to Illinois. Still, Poe hoped some day to meet Peters, and did not care to say to the public exactly where he could be met with. Then came Poe's unutterably sad death, leaving the narrative incomplete."

As Bainbridge neared the close of his remarks, we heard a heavy and rapid step approach along the hall. It stopped before my door; and just as Bainbridge ceased to speak, a loud rap, evidently made with the head of a heavy cane, sounded on the panel. The door flew open, and Doctor Castleton rushed into the middle of the room - or, rather, bounded across the room. Bainbridge and I instantly arose, and I stepped forward to take Doctor Castleton's hand in mine, and to care for his hat and cane; but he waved me off. "No, no: no time - not a minute to spare - three patients waiting" - here he glanced at Bainbridge, as if to observe the effect of his speech on a beginner, who was fortunate if he yet possessed a single patient - "like to keep my word - fine evening." He seated himself on the edge of a chair, and projected his glance around the room. No better subject immediately presenting itself to mind, I remarked that we had just been talking of Edgar Allan Poe, and his unfinished story, "The Narrative of A. Gordon Pym"; and I spoke of Dirk Peters.

"I know old man Peters - know him well, sir," said Doctor Castleton, without a moment's hesitation; "short old fellow - seafaring man - about four feet six, or seven - must have been a devil in his day - old man, now - seventy or eighty; no hair, no beard; farms a few acres on the Bluff; very sick man, right now."

Charles Romyn Dake

Bainbridge and I had cast at each other a glance, which plainly said, "Isn't that Castleton for you?" But as he continued, and we had time to consider, the probability that Dirk Peters was alive, and the bare possibility that he was in the neighborhood, and that, if he did reside near Bellevue, Doctor Castleton would be very likely to have met him, gradually dawned on our minds. Quick as was the glance we exchanged, Castleton saw it - yes, and understood it.

"Gentlemen," he continued, "I know whereof I speak. It is true, I never before thought of Peters in this connection. In the cases of my library, the books stand two rows deep. Thousands of books have been carried into my attic, to make room for newer books - I never need to glance twice at a book. Of course I have Poe's works, and bound in morocco, too - the grandest genius ever bestowed upon humanity by the prolific and liberal hand of our Creator. Still, I never happened to read the grand and mighty effort of that colossal intellect to which you refer - 'The Narrative of a Snorting Thing,' though I recall 'The Literary Life of Thingum Bob.' But I am certain - certain as the unerring fiat of Omnipotent Power - that this man Peters is within ten miles of us, and is at this moment a mighty ill man - almost ready, in fact, to visit a land from which he will be little likely to return. I refer to 'The undiscovered country from whose bourne no traveller returns.' By super-human efforts I have kept this man Peters alive now long past the time-limit set by his Creator for him to go - I mean, three score and ten years; but even I and science have our limitations, and the beginning of the end is at hand."

By this time Doctor Castleton was pacing up and down the room, stopping now and then to look at an engraving on the wall, taking up and replacing books, seeing everything. I could not but feel that already the curiosity which had impelled him to "run in" was satisfied, and that he would soon be going. A minute after his last recorded words, Dirk Peters seemed to have dropped completely from his mind. I was wholly absorbed with the thought that Dirk Peters might be within our reach; and that if he really was, it was possible that we might learn whether Pym and he had reached the South Pole, and if so, what they had there discovered. It was plainly evident that the mind of Doctor Bainbridge was deeply engaged with the same subject. I was anxious to know what he thought of Castleton's statement; for the more I discussed the matter within myself, the more I felt inclined to believe that Castleton was not making a mistake. But Castleton was certainly now not thinking of Peters. I could, amid my thoughts, hear him declaiming,

"Yes, sir; England is a mighty power. Her navy, sir, can - and mark me, it will - sweep France and Russia and Prussia and Austria and Italy from the ocean as - as a shar - a wha - a huge and voracious swordfish sweeps before its imperious onslaught, with unerring certainty and cyclonic power, a whole school of sneaking mackerel or codfish from the pathway fixed for it by Eternal Destiny."

His prognostication was intended to be a graceful compliment paid to the country of a visiting stranger, and, in the absence of other foreigners, not discourteous to anybody. I never before or since knew his natural flow of eloquence to waver as in this instance - a rarity that of itself makes the remark worthy of record. Doctor Castleton soon, against all protests, bounded out of the door, as he had bounded in; and then Bainbridge and I discussed the astonishing possibilities should it prove true that Dirk Peters was within our reach. We concluded that Castleton's statement was one of great importance, and we agreed upon a course of procedure. We spent the remainder of the evening in a manner very enjoyable to myself, and evidently gratifying to Doctor Bainbridge; and it was past midnight when we separated.

The following morning I looked up Doctor Castleton; and he, ever courteous and obliging, did more than consent to permit me to drive out to the home of his patient, Peters. He proposed that I wait a day, as he knew that Peters would within that time, and might any hour, send for him; and as soon as he was summoned he would notify me, and together we would drive out to the old sailor's residence - which, the doctor said, was a small, two-roomed log structure, where the old man dwelt entirely alone.

THE FOURTH CHAPTER

The summons from Doctor Castleton to accompany him came sooner than he had led me to expect; and at a little past noon of the same day on which he had made his promise to take me with him to see Dirk Peters, I received a message, saying that if agreeable to me he would at two o'clock be in front of my hotel, prepared to start for the home of the old sailor.

At a minute or two before the time fixed, I was standing at the main entrance to the Loomis House, and at precisely two o'clock Doctor Castleton drove up in a two-horse, four-wheeled, top-buggy. He made room for me on his left, and off we started.

We drove in a westerly direction for a full mile along the main street before leaving the town behind us. Then we struck a level turf road; and away trotted the superb team of rather small, wiry, black horses. Doctor Castleton said that we should reach our destination - which was rather more than ten miles from the city limits - within forty minutes; and we did. Over a part of the level turf road I should estimate that we drove at about a three-minute gait; but after traversing some four or five miles, we turned south into a narrow road, which soon became hilly and tortuous; yet even here it was only on particularly rough or uneven portions of the way that the doctor moderated our speed to less than a four-minute gait.

As we rode along at this exhilarating pace, the buggy whirling around acute curves among the mighty oaks and maples, now

Charles Romyn Dake

and then dashing down a forty-five-degree descent of fifty or sixty feet, again thundering over a dilapidated bridge of resonant planks, the doctor remarked to me that Peters was certain to die, it being only a question of days, or perhaps of hours. "Old Peters," he said, "has been without visible means of support for the past two or three years. The Lord only knows how he has lived since the period when he became unable to work. Even his small farm is mortgaged for all it is worth." I expressed to the doctor some surprise that he should be making twenty-mile drives to see a lonely old man whose illness he was unable to relieve, and from whom he could expect no fee. I had grown to take an interest in hearing Castleton express his opinions. Many of his conceptions of life were so unique; his mental vision, always intensely acute, was often so oblique; his station of mental observation so alterable, and so quickly altered; his sentiments often so earthy, again so exalted - that I believe the man would have interested me even under circumstances less quiet and monotonous than were those of my stay, up to this time, in Bellevue. To my expression of mild wonderment that he should tax his time and energies to such an extent without pecuniary gain, he replied:

"My dear sir, you are a traveller. You have sailed the seas and crossed the mighty main; you have dashed over mountains, and sweltered 'mid tropical suns on sandy desert-wastes. To you our Rockies are mole-hills - our great lakes mere ponds. You are not a child to cry out in the darkness. Granted. Yet, sir, let us by a stretch of fancy imagine ourselves in the place of Columbus, on the third day of August, 1492. We are about to leave the Known, in search of the Unknown - about to penetrate for the first time that vast expanse of water which for uncounted ages has stretched away before the wondering vision and baffled research of Europe. We are not leaving the world - we are not alone. Yet is it not a solace that a few friends gather on the shore to say good-by? The sympathy of the kind, the well-wishes of the brave - are they not always a comfort? This poor fellow Peters, whose lowly home we are now approaching, is alone - he is about to start on his last journey, alone. The land to which he perhaps this day begins that journey is not only unknown, but unknowable to us in our present state. And therefore is it, sir, that the learned professions live. Even the worldly man, when he comes to start upon this last journey, does not disdain the sympathy and kindness of the loving, and the expressions of hopefulness that come from the good and pure. True, you may say that the learned professions are for the man who is about to die but frail supports on which to lean. The wise man as well as the ignorant man, when he fears that death is near, reaches out for help or at least some knowledge of his future. He sends for his physician, who cannot promise him anything - cannot number the days or hours of his remaining life; for his lawyer, who cannot assure him beyond all doubt that his will can be made to endure for a single day beyond his death. At last, he sends for a minister of God - and what says the spiritual expert? Perhaps he represents that old, old organization, whose history stretches back for centuries through the dark ages to the borders of the brilliancy beyond; that old hierarchy that claims to hold all spiritual power to which man may appeal with reasonable hope. What says to the dying man this representative and heir of the accumulated spiritual research and culture of the past? He may with honesty say, 'Hope;' but if he says more than Hope, he does it as the blind might sit and guide by signs through unknown labyrinths the blind. All this is true; but the fact that the learned professions have come into existence, and continue to live and draw from the masses their material support - a tax greater in amount than the income of the nations - shows that they meet, and genuinely meet, a demand. I say genuinely, for 'You cannot fool all the people all the time.' And so, my young friend, this poor man Peters wants me. Later, if there is time, he will want the representative of the religion which he professes, or which he remembers that his mother or his father professed. I shall stand by his side and place my hand upon his throbbing brow - and he will hope, and not despair. Who knows whether or not our hope and our faith have power in some strange way to link the present to the future, carrying forward the spirit-seed to soil in which it blooms in splendor through eternity? As Byron says,

Charles Romyn Dake

'How little do we know that which we are,
How less what we may be.'

But here we are; and I know by the face of that old neighbor-woman looking from the doorway there that our man still lives."

We drew up in front of a small building some sixteen feet square, the walls of which consisted of huge logs piled one upon another and mortised at the corners. The doctor entered, leaving me seated in the buggy. But soon he came to the door, and signalled for me. As I entered the house I heard a voice say, "Yes, doctor, the old hulk's still afloat - water-logged, but still afloat." Looking in the direction of the voice, I saw on a bed in one corner of the room an old beardless man. I had not a second's doubt that Dirk Peters of the 'Grampus,' sailor, mutineer, explorer of the Antarctic Sea, patron and friend of A. Gordon Pym, was before me. His body up to the waist was covered with an old blanket; but I felt certain that he was less than five feet in height, and felt quite positive that he would not then measure more than four and a half feet. His height in 1827 was, Poe states, four feet and eight inches. One of the old man's arms lay exposed by his side, and the finger-ends reached below the knee; while his hand, spread out on the blanket, would have covered the area of a small ham. His shoulders and neck, and the one bare arm visible, were indicative of vast muscular strength. There was the enormous head mentioned by Poe; and there was the completely bald scalp, exposed, as by a semi-automatic movement of respect he raised his hand to his head and removed a section of woolly sheepskin; and there, too, was the indenture in the crown; there the enormous mouth, spreading from ear to ear, with the lips which, as he gave a chuckle, and the wrinkles about his eyes evinced a passing facial contortion, I saw to be wholly wanting in pliancy. There was the expression, fixed at least as far as the mouth and lower face was concerned, the protruding teeth, and the grotesque appearance of a smile such as a demon might have smiled over ruined innocence. Oh, there was no possibility of a mistake. Doctor Castleton glanced at me questioningly, but confidently; and I lowered my head in assent. But if I expected to have an opportunity of learning much of anything from Peters, I was mistaken. Doctor Castleton was almost ready to depart before I had finished my visual examination of the old man. I heard the aged neighbor-woman, a coal miner's wife, who had as an act of kindness come in to assist the invalid, say, looking at the poor old fellow:

"My mon stayed wi' he the night, dochter. The poor mon, he had delerion bad. He thot hesel' on a mountain o' ice, wi' tha mountain o' ice on other like mountain o' salt, a lookin' at devils i' hell. But sin' tha light o' day. Tha good mon's hesel' agin."

Doctor Castleton had produced from the recesses of a large medicine case certain pills and powders, had given his directions, and was actually about to leave without giving me an opportunity, or seeming to think that I desired an opportunity, of speaking with Peters. I then appealed for a moment more of time, and for consent to ask the patient a question or two; and my appeal was granted. I stepped close to the bedside, and looking down into the eyes that looked up into mine, asked the old man if his name was Dirk Peters; to which he answered affirmatively. I then asked him if he had in the year 1827 sailed from the port of Nantucket, on the brig 'Grampus,' under Captain Bernard, in company, among others, with a youth named A. Gordon Pym? And a moment later I wished that I had been less abrupt in my questioning. Peters did manage quite coolly and rationally to answer "Yes" to all my questions. But at the words "Pym," "Bernard," "Grampus," his eyes began, in appearance, to start from their sockets; those awful teeth gleamed from that cavernous mouth, as he uttered demoniac yell on yell, and raised himself to a sitting posture in the bed. I thought his eyeballs must certainly burst, as he looked off into nothingness wildly, as if a troop of fiends were rushing upon him.

"Great God!" he screamed, "there, there - she's gone. Ah,"

quieting a little; "ah; the old man with the eyes of a god, and the cubes of crystal with the limpid liquid of heaven. Oh," his voice again raised to piercing screams, "Oh, she's gone, and he loves her - and I love him. Now man, they called you the human baboon - be more than man! - I loved the boy - I tell you, I loved him from the first. I saved him once - aye, a dozen times - but not like this - not from hell. Scale the chasms of salt, and climb the lava cliffs, and - but the lake of fire at the bottom - the old man - and the abyss, my God, the abyss! The snow-drift beard - the godlike eyes" - his voice then quieting for a few words. 'Ah, mother, mother, mother." Then in a deep, earnest tone, "I'll be a human baboon, and I'll do what man never yet did, nor beast - yes, and what never in time will man do again."

Then he completely lost control of himself. He jumped from the bed. Doctor Castleton stood near the doorway, and I quickly moved to his side. The old woman had vanished. Peters poured forth yell on yell, such as I had never conceived it possible for a human throat to utter. He grasped a strong oak-pole, and broke it as I might have broken a dry twig. I afterward placed the longer fragment of this pole with each of its extremities on a large stone, the two about four feet apart; and lifting into the air a rock weighing a hundred or more pounds, dropped it on the middle of the fragment; and it did not even bend what this man of awful strength had severed with his two hands as one would break a wooden toothpick between the fingers. Then Peters picked up a stove which stood, fireless, in the room; and he cast it through an open window, seven or eight feet away, into the yard beyond, where it fell, breaking into a hundred pieces. I need scarcely say that Doctor Castleton and myself had left the room with decided alacrity. Well, to terminate a description none too agreeable, Peters' wild delirium continued until, out in the door-yard, forty or fifty feet from the house, he fell, exhausted. Then we carried him back to his bed. Doctor Castleton gave some directions to the old woman, and soon we left for town, Peters being asleep.

"Strange," said Doctor Castleton, after we had driven for perhaps a mile, "strange that a thought can do such things! A word is said, the thread of memory is touched by suggestion, and it vibrates back through half a century to some scene of terror stamped ineradicably upon the brain - or if not upon the brain, then where? - and, lo! the reflexes spring into action, and a maniac with Samson's strength takes the place of a docile invalid. Ah, who can answer the mystery of mysteries, and tell us what this consciousness is! Behind that gift of God rests the secret of life, and of death, and probably of Eternity itself."

We rode along, returning a little more leisurely than we had come. I sat wondering how we were to learn from such a man as Peters his secrets - if secrets he possessed. Even if his past held only important facts not of secret import, I had received striking evidence that the subject of that wonderful sea-voyage was not to be carelessly broached to Dirk Peters. I concluded to say nothing more of the matter until I should meet Bainbridge, whom I knew would be anxiously awaiting my return, hardly daring to hope that Poe's Dirk Peters was really in existence and discovered.

As we neared town, my mind turned to the strange being at my side. Here was a man who could think, and think both learnedly and poetically of the wonders of heaven and earth; and yet who could talk of driving from town a business competitor! Surely that part of his talk which seemed so laughable was in spirit wholly dramatic - intended rather to fill the assumed expectations of his hearers, than truly representing the speaker's feeling. Then my thoughts reverted to the talk I had overheard, when "Pickles" was made to see veritable showers of "greenbacks" raining into his vacuous pocket. I smiled to myself; and then a spirit of audacity coming over me, I determined to ascertain what Castleton would say to me on the currency question. I concluded to admit that I had overheard through my open window the conversation on monetary matters alluded to. There would then be no opportunity for him to evade the responsibility of assuming as his own the peculiar opinions expressed by him on that occasion. Now, when he could not consistently deny the advocacy of views to me so apparently untenable, and could not seriously adopt them without lowering himself intellectually in the estimation of a stranger - and I did not for an instant think that he believed the nonsense which he had so glowingly represented and demonstrated to poor old "Pickles" - then by what possible means would he extricate himself from the dilemma?

When I broached the money question, he seemed to warm to the subject at once; but as I led around to the fact of my overhearing the "Pickles" incident, he seemed slightly disconcerted - but only momentarily. He was himself again so quickly that I should not have noticed his embarrassment had I not been closely observing him for that very purpose.

"Well, now," he said, blithely, "as you are a stranger, a man of high and irreproachable honor, *sans peur et sans reproche* - and one, I know, who will not place me in an equivocal position here in my home by divulging my true position - I don't mind telling you, in all confidence, the truth. I am not, my dear sir, an ass. (What I say, remember, goes no farther.) I am, sir, a theoretical and practical politician of great - I only repeat what many of my friends (men of supreme mental attainments, and the best of judges) herald forth as undeniable truth - a politician, sir, of great depth and exceeding cunning - a rare combination, philosophers tell us. What a humbug this whole greenback question is! Why, sir, it is to that very element of scarcity over which they howl, that money, or anything else, owes its commercial value. Diminish the general scarcity of anything on earth to the point of a full supply for everybody and the commercial value at once becomes *nil.* There is nothing of more real value than atmospheric air; yet the supply is so great that all demands are filled, leaving an enormous surplus; and hence atmospheric air has no commercial value. There is nothing on earth of much less service to humanity than are diamonds; yet the possession of a pound of fair-sized diamonds would make a Croesus of a beggar. The dreams of the Greenbacker are but new phases of our childhood fancies of finding a mountain of pure gold, with which we are to make the whole world happy; it is conceivable to find the mountain of gold - but, alas! what will be its value when we have found it? Take actual money, for instance. Any metal might be used as money which the world should agree to call money, provided only that the metal is not so plentiful as to make it impossible to handle because of bulk, or so scarce as to make the unit of value impalpable. The standard may even from time to time be changed, if we do not object to the enormous trouble of making the change -"

"And," I remarked, as he paused for a moment, "if we do not object to the robbery of either the debtor or the creditor, one or the other."

"Not at all," he replied. "I assume that the change shall be fairly made. I have said that it would be a very great inconvenience to the world, and without any benefit; it would in fact be so great a task to make the change in our money standard that it would be practically impossible to make it. But we are off the track - we were not to talk of primary money; it was of currency, or greenbacks, that you spoke. Now it puzzles you as a man of sense to conceive by what process of thought another man of sense can bring himself to advocate unlimited inflation of our currency; and yet there is a very good reason why the most sensible man may do that very thing. Of course, my dear sir, I am aware that the only honest way for a government to issue unlimited currency is to give the stuff away, and later to repudiate it. Now, sir, I need not tell one like yourself, who has studied the lives of such English statesmen as the puissant Burke, the sagacious Pitt, the astute Palmerston, that ninety per cent, of the people - and it is so even in this glorious land of free schools and liberty - are relatively to the remaining ten per cent, either poor and dishonest, or poor and ignorant; and that none of the hundred per cent, goes into sackcloth and ashes when he gets something for nothing. I, sir, am - or I was until recently - a Jeffersonian Democrat. But our party made a great mistake a few years ago by sticking to the slave interest too long. I finally became

Charles Romyn Dake

hopeless of success at the polls. Now, when I whisper in your all-comprehending ear that the leaders of this Greenback Party are anything but Republicans, you will grasp the point. I repeat, sir, I am not an ass - if I do bray sometimes. All's fair in love and politics. But let me say to you, that the printing presses of the United States will never be leased by the United States Treasury, whatever party wins at the polls."

As he closed, we entered the town. It may not be wholly lacking in interest to the reader when I say that, some years later, as I one morning sat in my library looking through the window at the far-distant smoke of Newcastle, I had just laid aside a copy of the *Times*, in which paper I had read of the results of a political contest in the State of Illinois. The Republicans had won. The Greenbackers and the Democrats had lost. Then my eye caught the name of Castleton! The doctor had made the race for Governor - not on the Greenback ticket, however; not on the Democratic ticket; but - of all things! - on the *anti-liquor or Prohibition ticket!*

As we drew up in front of the Loomis House, Doctor Bainbridge stood on the sidewalk as if awaiting our return. I smiled, then nodded an affirmative to the question in his eyes; and stepping out of the buggy, I linked his arm within my own, and, thanking Doctor Castleton for his kindness, piloted the way to my room.

THE FIFTH CHAPTER

On opening the door of my sitting-room, I found Arthur, the factotum, sitting in my large easy-chair, with one of my volumes of Poe in his hand. He had overheard part of the conversation of the preceding evening, and was evidently interested in "The Narrative of A. Gordon Pym." I observed also that a bottle of cognac which sat upon my table, and which I could have sworn was not more than one-fourth emptied when I left the hotel directly after dinner, was now quite empty. The atmosphere of the room was pervaded with the odor of "dead" brandy; and Arthur's eyes were unusually glassy and staring - for so early an hour as 5 P.M. Then he settled the matter, beyond the shadow of a doubt, with a hiccough.

"Well, Arthur," I said, pleasantly, as he clumsily rose in part from his seat - into which he dropped back, however, as he heard my kindly tone of address, and knew there was to be no severity of reckoning - "well, my boy; been enjoying yourself?"

"Yes, sir," he replied, in a fairly steady voice - the words that followed, however, being rhythmically interrupted by an aldermanic and most vociferous hiccough, which shall be omitted from this record - "been reading about Pym and Barnard. Wasn't that awful when they saw the shipful of dead corpses? Just think of that ship, full of dead men - not one of them alive, and all dead - and the sails set, and the old ship wabbling around the ocean just as things might please to happen! When the ship got close up to their brig, and that

Charles Romyn Dake

scream came from among the corpses, I just jumped, myself! But wasn't it terrible when that gull pulled its bloody old beak out of the dead man's back, and then flew over the brig and dropped the piece of human flesh at poor hungry Parker's feet? Gee-whillikens, now! Why, it just made my blood sink in my heart and lungs."

"Yes," I thought, "and it just made my brandy sink pretty fast in my bottle and down your throat." I was amused at his comments, and at another time might have listened longer to his talk; but now I must be making some arrangement with Doctor Bainbridge regarding a possible interview with Peters; so I said to Arthur that he might take the volume of Poe and keep it for two or three days, which offer he gladly accepted; and with an involuntary wandering of the eye toward the brandy bottle, he left the room.

Then Bainbridge and I seated ourselves, and I described the late scene in Dirk Peters' room, repeating almost word for word all that had been said. He pondered for a few minutes, during which I could see that his versatile imagination was in active play. Then he said,

"Well, we have him! My, my, what a discovery! This will be like reaching across the decrees of death and taking by the hand dear Poe himself! But you were hasty - as I myself might have been. Well, we must see Castleton - that is, you must - and get his consent for us to go right out and stay with Peters, if necessary for a night and a day, or even longer. We can take care of the poor old fellow, and watch our opportunity to glean from him the facts of that strange voyage, onward from the moment when, borne on that swift ocean current, he and Pym were rushed into the mystery that opened to receive them, as the white-shrouded figure arose in their pathway. 'Fire' - 'salt' - 'ice,' said he? I begin almost - almost to understand! Did you ever, in England, hear of the Peruvian tradition of an antarctic country, warm and delightful, peopled by a civilized - or rather by a highly enlightened and very mysterious race of whites? Such a tradition exists. Now, one day in New York, about three years ago, I allowed myself a holiday, as was my custom from time to time after a period of severe study. On the day I speak of I entered the Astor Library, and was permitted to wander at my pleasure among the books. I carried in my hand one of the small camp-stools which stood around the room, and whenever I found a book that particularly interested me, I would sit down and look it over. You understand, I was dissipating in this great treasure-house of books. About the middle of the afternoon I found myself in one of the most unfrequented of the library alcoves. There, on a shelf so high that I could just see over its edge as I stood on one of the library step-ladders, I found a strange little book, purporting to have been written in 1594. It had fallen down behind the other books. It had a leather back, well-worn; I saw that it was a 1728 Leipsic publication; and possibly came to the Astor Library by presentation from its wise and liberal founder's private library - though this is pure surmise. The book read much like other tales of the time, so far as its form went. I sat down to look at it - and I did not arise until I had read it to its end, some three hours later. I had not read two pages before I became satisfied that the book had more truth than fiction in it. To have assumed it wholly the work of imagination, I should have had to admit that the author was an artist of artists, exceeding, through his artfulness, in naturalness, all other fiction-writers. No; there was truth behind the statements in the little book - truth at second or third hand, but truth. Now this little book pretended to tell, and I believe did tell, the story of a sailor under Sir Francis Drake, who accompanied this English navigator on his 1577-1580 voyage. You will recall, as a matter of history, that, in the voyage mentioned, Sir Francis crossed the Atlantic, passed the Strait of Magellan, crossed the Pacific, and returned to England by way of the Cape of Good Hope. Now during this three-year voyage, the story is that he once lost his 'bearings' for a month; in fact, it is intimated that a hiatus of two months in his 'log' really did exist. This hiatus, however, could easily have been covered in the ship's log-book. We may conceive of reasons for which he might have preferred to keep a temporary silence concerning the discovery of a strange people, in those

Charles Romyn Dake

early, savage times. The little book said, that, when in the Pacific, after passing the strait, Sir Francis was for two weeks driven in a southerly course - a severe, and in every way most unusual storm prevailing. When the winds and the waves subsided, he was surprised to find himself looking into the mouth of a harbor, on the shores of which stood a city, by no means so large as London or even as Paris; but exceeding in grandeur the London or the Paris of that day, as the Paris of to-day exceeds in elegance the comparative squalor of the Paris of three centuries ago. According to the leather-covered little German book, the city was beautiful beyond comparison with any of the European cities of that period. I should suppose that the author thought of it as we do of Athens in the days of Pericles. Not much is said of the inhabitants, who were probably infinitely superior, socially, to the rough voyagers of that date. And for once the 'natives' were neither bullied nor 'converted,' Sir Francis departing no richer than he arrived, save for a few commercially valueless gifts. One thing the natives, it seems, insisted on: Sir Francis arrived in the city without knowing his longitude; and they compelled him on leaving to accept conditions that prevented him from finding his bearings till he was more than a thousand miles away. What the nature of the climate was in this strange city may be judged by the expressions employed in the little book, which, translated, were equivalent to 'perfect,' 'Eden-like,' 'balmy,' 'delicious.' Once the author compares this antarctic city to Venice - admittedly to the Venice of his imagination. No; Sir Francis had nothing to brag of in this adventure; and in those days when to be physically subdued, or in a contest to fail to subdue others, was a humiliation or even a disgrace, he would have kept very quiet about the whole affair; particularly as a future navigator could not have found the city, even had Sir Francis told all that he knew. Now I mention these reports only to show you that others have thought of warm antarctic lands; and I could refer you to many other old stories and traditions, highly suggestive of inhabited lands in the Antarctic Ocean, on which lands a refined people dwell. I certainly expect to learn from Peters facts of some importance to the world, if only he does not die, or is not so delirious as to throw a shadow on the verity of his story, even if he does disclose the wonders which I most assuredly believe that he will if he lives but another day. Really, I am, for the first time in years, excited. How Castleton keeps so cool and so apparently indifferent over this matter, when he is always excited over what seem to me to be comparative nothings, I cannot comprehend. Now, sir, you hunt him up again - he will no doubt be in his office across the street. Get his consent, as I before suggested - Castleton is always obliging when you appeal to him directly; then take your supper, and be ready. I will be here at eight o'clock with my horse and a piano-box buggy. It will be a beautiful moonlight night, and let us not risk waiting until to-morrow. We will take with us some ice; also wine, beef extract, and a few other things intended to sustain the poor old fellow's vitality - at least till his story is told. We must go prepared to remain for twenty-four hours, or even for thirty-six hours if necessary; so have your overcoat ready, and I will find a couple of blankets in case we have to lie down. Good-by till eight."

And off he went, as excited as a schoolboy at the beginning of an adventure. I began to think he was allowing his imaginations to pray him tricks - purposely allowing himself to be deceived, as a child that is nearing the age of reason still delights in the old fairy tales and the Santa Claus myth, long after its mind has penetrated the deception. Still, in the end it proved we were very far - very far indeed from being upon an idle quest.

By eight o'clock I had obtained Doctor Castleton's consent that Bainbridge and I might visit Peters, and remain as long as we should desire.

"I will run out myself, early in the morning," said Castleton, "and do what I can to keep life in the old man. Don't let Bainbridge get into the old fellow any of his newfangled, highfalutin remedies - if you do, I will not answer for the consequences. I don't say that Bainbridge will not in time - in time, mark you - be a dazzling therapeutist; but not until experience has modified his views, and shown him that Rome was not built in a day, nor with a toothpick, either. Don't tell him what I say, please - I wouldn't like to hurt his young feelings, you know."

When Doctor Bainbridge drove up in front of the hotel, I was waiting for him; and we were soon on our way toward the Peters domicile.

THE SIXTH CHAPTER

The time required by Doctor Castleton to reach the home of Dirk Peters had been about forty minutes; the time required by Doctor Bainbridge was two and one-half times forty minutes, or only twenty minutes short of two hours. Bainbridge drove a single horse, a beautiful, large, dappled bay - an excellent animal, which, as most horses do, had learned those of his master's ways that bore relation to his own interests. Bainbridge was a lover of animals, as Castleton was not; Castleton was an admirer of horses for their action, whilst with Bainbridge the welfare of his horse was everything, and he never drove rapidly without a particular and pressing necessity.

So we drove along in a leisurely way, conversing of Dirk Peters and the Pym story, until we had arranged a plan of action for drawing out of the old man an account of that voyage, the mere thought of which, coming suddenly upon him, had affected him in the terrible manner which I had that afternoon witnessed. Doctor Bainbridge explained to me that the wild demonstrations made by Peters and described by me were a result, not so much of any thought of those adventures on which he must have pondered thousands of times in the forty-eight or forty-nine intervening years, as it was of the manner in which the thoughts or mental pictures had been brought to his mind.

"I need only remind you," he said, "of a single mental characteristic within the experience of almost every person, to make this matter clear, and to indicate what our course with

Charles Romyn Dake

the old man must be, and why I said to you to come prepared for a long stay. Suppose, for instance, a woman to have lost her husband through some extremely painful accident, his death being not only sudden but of a horrifying nature, and that several years have elapsed since she was widowed. Now, she has thought the matter over ten thousand times, as the suggestion to do so entered her mind by a hundred different routes, as, for instance, by the seeing of something that her husband in life possessed, or by the drift of her own thought bringing her to the subject by association or by indirect paths of suggestion. Every day her mind has many times pictured the horrible scene of death, until she is cry-eyed and passive amid a storm of sad ideas. But now, after all these years, bring to her mind, suddenly and by a strange route of suggestion, the same old horror - let a voice, and particularly the voice of a stranger, remind her of the terrible scene - and immediately the demonstration follows: the sobs of anguish, the tears, all, as on the day of the accident. It is the method of approach - the mode of suggestion when the fact is known but latent in consciousness, that is responsible for the nervous demonstration. In another instance, visual suggestion might have a similar result and audible suggestion be harmless. I anticipate no serious obstruction in the path to Peters' confidence. Patience, care, deliberate action - the fact ever in mind that 'The more haste the less speed,' and we shall win the prize for which we strive."

As we drove along in the bright moonlight, after we had determined on our "method of approach" to Peters' mind, I felt confident that with the knowledge and tact of Bainbridge we should certainly succeed in our efforts; and I began to think along other lines. The friendly manner in which I had been treated by all whom I had met in America, from the millionaire coal operator down to the bell-boy, came into my thoughts. I had not been treated as a foreigner, except to my own advantage, the older residents of the town seeming to look upon me more as they might look upon a man from another State of the Union. In America, even the inland towns are cosmopolitan, while in England only the larger cities and seaport towns have that characteristic. I was therefore able to judge of certain questions not only from hearsay, but from actual observation. I noticed, for example, that among the American working-classes there existed a feeling of repugnance for the Chinaman. Of the lower-class Italian, everybody thought enough to keep out of his reach after dark. Germans and Irishmen were numerous, and each individual was taken on his own merits. The English were universally liked, wherever I went. True, there was a little tendency to allude to the glories of Bunker Hill and the like; but this tendency was evinced in a manner rather amusing than objectionable to an Englishman. If there exists in the American heart a drop of bitterness for the English, I never discovered it. I am writing now of the American-born American. I gathered the idea that Frenchmen, as seen in America, were scarcely taken seriously; though all Americans have been systematically educated to respect and admire the French Nation. Of Spaniards, the prevalent idea seemed to be that they were better at arm's length. (Anglo-Saxon literature has been very unkind to the Spaniard.) I did not meet an American that seemed to hate anybody - I do not conceive it possible for an American to harbor the feeling of hatred.

As we jogged along, the idea entered my mind that I would, when I returned home, write a treatise on "American Manners and Customs." "No doubt," I said to myself, "I can in the next few minutes procure from Bainbridge enough facts to make quite a book." I afterward abandoned the intention; but at that moment my mind was filled with it. So I decided to ask my companion a few leading questions, noting well his replies. "And I will first," I determined within myself, "inquire into the mooted point concerning the existence of an aristocratic feeling in the United States. Some of our English writers on 'American Manners and Customs,' and our most acute analysts of American character, say that the Americans are great snobs, and are only too glad to claim the possession of even the most distant aristocratic connection;" so I broached the subject to Bainbridge.

"It interests me to convince you," he began, in reply, "that in the United States there is scarcely a vestige of aristocratic feeling. In fact as in theory, there is in this country but one class of people. Such supposed barriers as wealth and political position are only partitions of paper - relative nothings. I do not mention heredity, because in the United States all attempts to establish a family line result in the family rotting before it gets ripe. The only pretence to hereditary pride which we have here, exists in two States; in one of them some four or five hundred persons cannot forget that their forefathers got to shore before somebody else; and in the other a few families still dispute over the threadbare question of whose great-great-grandmother cost the most pounds of tobacco. Now, candidly - is this sufficient to justify a reproach from Europe that we are striving to claim or to create an aristocracy?

"And then there is that other reproach - we're such outrageous tuft-hunters. I shall not deny having seen an American run himself out of breath to get a peep at a duke, but I never knew an American spend money to see one, unless the American was too beastly rich to care for money at all. And then, hereditary nobles do not wear well here. Let a visiting duke be followed within a year by anything less than a king, and the visitor will fail to excite anybody out of a walk. You must not in England judge of this subject from the effect on our people of a certain not remote visit; for the people of the United States have a feeling of respect and affection for the present royal family of Great Britain which no other royal family or individual, past or present, has ever produced. Hum, hum! Our people mean well; but curiosity and imitation will not die out of the human race till an inch or two more of the spinal column drops off."

Still with a view to the gathering of facts for my intended treatise, I asked Bainbridge to explain in what distinctive manner the people of the United States were benefited by a republican form of government. He replied that he knew nothing worth mentioning of the science of government, and had never been outside of the United States.

"But," he continued, "I can tell you something of what the whole people of this country enjoy. And to begin with, there is, as I have intimated, in the United States but one class of people, aside from the criminal class common to all lands, and that vicious but not relatively numerous element which lives on the borderland between respectability and actual crime. This truth seems sometimes to be questioned in Europe - why, I can but guess. Who would attempt to enter the nurseries and schoolrooms of our land today, and, by inquiring as to the parentage of the children, select from among them any approximation to those from whom are to come, in twenty or thirty years, the men that shall then govern our States, sit in our National Congress, direct our army and navy, and control our commerce? I have heard that in Europe it is rather the exception for a son to reach exalted position when the father has earned a living by manual labor. In the United States this is not the exception, but the rule. At this moment the positions alluded to are here filled by the sons of poor fathers. With us, inherited wealth appears to be rather a detriment than an aid to political advancement of more than a petty kind. 'And yet,' you may say, 'your people are not always satisfied.' No advancing, upward-looking people is ever satisfied. With such a people, too, the demagogue is a natural product; and the demagogue period of this country is at hand. But there will never be a tom-fool revolution in this fair land. The people here know that when they have universal suffrage and majority rule they've pulled the last hair out of the end of the cat's tail for them."

I made a remark, to which Bainbridge replied:

"Yes, we managed to finish up a pretty fair revolution here some twelve years ago; but that revolution was caused by a disagreement about the R. of B. Now -"

"Pardon me," I said "but what was the 'R. of B?'"

"Oh, excuse me," he answered. "The R. of B. was the Relic of Barbarism, human slavery - the only relic the United States has ever had, too."

I prided myself that the material for my book was piling up at a great rate; and I determined to persevere.

"How about the feeling of dislike of Americans for the English, of which we have heard so much in England?" I asked. "Not that I have had any evidence of such a feeling."

"That is a plant which has finally withered away in spite of some careful artificial cultivation. The politician who shall attempt to build on any such feeling against England (a statesman will never desire to make the attempt) will soon learn his mistake. Oh, I suppose it pleases some Americans to think we got the best of our mother in 1783 - such a big, strong, wealthy mother, too. A little bit of talk doesn't hurt her any, and it does some of us a heap of good. When a boy runs away from home, half the glory and fun is in being missed; and if the folks at home won't say they miss him, why, he must say all the louder that they are mourning over the loss. But I will say to you - and I say it with the fullest conviction of its truth - that the people of the United States could not in any way be induced to take up arms against Great Britain, save in their own undivided interest. Individually, as you already know, I love England - not England's fops, but her people; I love the literature of England, I love her memories, I esteem and admire her well-executed laws. The literature of England has been my mental food from boyhood - aye, almost from infancy; and her memories, her memories! I think of London as Macaulay must have thought of Athens. Decent Americans - that is, a majority - don't listen to jingo politicians; and new arrivals with a grievance against England are left to the *vis medicatrix naturae*. There'll never be another war between England and the United States. Our Anglo-Saxon element think normally; and the vast majority of our German citizens have always been on the sensible and morally right side of national questions - there's nothing long-haired or cranky about them. I like the Germans because they don't hanker after the unknown. I believe that most reading Americans -

that is to say three-fourths of all - feel toward England as Irving and Hawthorne did. - But, from your description, that must be the home of Peters, just ahead of us."

He was right; and we stopped in front of the old sailor's house. An aged man, apparently a coal miner, came to the door as our buggy stopped. We called him to us and inquired concerning Peters, who he told us was quietly sleeping. Then we asked with regard to stabling accommodations, and learned that Peters had an old unused stable, the last old horse that he had owned having preceded its master into the beyond. The old miner offered to care for our horse; so we gathered up our supplies, and entered the little log house that contained so much of interest for us. We found Peters asleep.

Making ourselves as comfortable as circumstances would permit, we awaited developments. At about midnight Peters awoke. He asked for a drink of water, which was given to him. His voice was feeble, and I saw that Bainbridge felt doubtful as to the length of time that Peters might remain alive and be able to talk intelligently. But after we had given him a little diluted port, and followed it with a cup of prepared beef extract, his actions betokened less weakness, his voice in particular gaining in strength. The poor old fellow had been of necessity much neglected, and our efforts to arouse him met with decidedly good results. All through the night we gratified every want which he expressed, and attended to every need of his that our own minds could suggest. No attempt was made to draw from him any information concerning his strange voyage; but, on the advice of Bainbridge, we occasionally spoke aloud to each other, and now and then to Peters himself - always on indifferent topics. This was done to familiarize the old sailor with our voices; and as far as we could do so without any possible injury to him, we kept a light in the room, that he should become accustomed to our appearance. From time to time Bainbridge would step to the bedside, and place his hand on the old man's forehead; and later he would every now and then put an arm about the invalid's body, and raise him up to take a swallow of nourishment or wine.

Charles Romyn Dake

Before morning, Bainbridge had reached a stage of familiarity that permitted him to sit on the edge of Peters' bed and talk to the old fellow briefly and quietly about his farm, and of Doctor Castleton's goodness and ability, and on other subjects presumably interesting to the invalid. Bainbridge would gently pat the poor old man on a shoulder, and smooth his head – somewhat as one does in making the acquaintance of a big dog. By morning Peters was thoroughly accustomed to our presence; and he seemed to take our watchfulness as a matter of course, and even to look for our attentions as a kind of right. He had slept several hours through the night, and at five o'clock was awake and seemingly much improved. Not the slightest delirium, even of the passive form - in fact, nothing of a nature that could alarm or disconcert us, had occurred. Bainbridge had mentioned eight o'clock as about the time he would broach the subject of subjects to Peters, intending, as a matter of course, to lead up to it by very tactful gradations, passing from journeys in the abstract to the journeys in the concrete, thence to sea voyages, and thence, perhaps, to some mention of recent arctic (not antarctic) explorations; and then, asking no questions yet, to proceed to a mention of Nantucket, from which vantage ground the propriety of risking a mention of the name Barnard would be considered. If up to this point all went well, a more pointed question or allusion might well be risked - the brig Grampus, for instance, might be named; and then, without more delay than should be necessary for Peters' rest, we might hope to elicit the whole story of that wonderful voyage of discovery, the evidence of the completion of which certainly appeared to be before our eyes in the form of Dirk Peters, the returned voyager to the South Pole, in person.

At six o'clock we prepared our own breakfast, and enjoyed it, sweetened as it was by a night in the pure country air, and seasoned with the anticipation of marvellous discoveries, involving the mysteries of a strange land, no doubt teeming with amazing surprises, and, as we felt that we had reason to believe, peopled by a race of beings with customs and attributes extremely wonderful.

We had just arisen from our breakfast when a buggy drove rapidly up to the house, and stopped; and we heard the voice of Doctor Castleton, shouting something to the old miner, who had gone forth a moment before to care for Bainbridge's horse.

THE SEVENTH CHAPTER

Doctor Castleton entered the sick-room with his usual impetuosity, saluting us jointly in an off-hand but courteous manner as he crossed the floor to the bedside of Peters, and took one of the invalid's wrists in his hand.

"Ah," he said; "better! The quinine of yesterday has done its work; the bed-time dose of calomel has gone through the liver and stirred up that enemy of human health and happiness, the bile; and the morning dose of salts will, beyond a peradventure, soon be heard from. Now we will throw the whiskey toddy into him, and plenty of it, too; and - yes, we'll go on with the quinine, repeat the calomel to-night, and have him ready for something else by to-morrow."

Now I never like to mention doubtful incidents in such a manner as to suggest my own belief in them; but I then suspected, and I am now morally certain, that Doctor Bainbridge had, in assuming the care of Peters, failed to execute medical orders, and had administered only remedies or pretended remedies of his own, so as to prevent Peters, myself, and the attending physician from detecting any omissions. This, I am aware, is a terrible charge to make - still, I make it: Peters did not get a fourth, if any, of the medicines left for him by Doctor Castleton during the time that Bainbridge cared for the old man.

But if Bainbridge had, with the intention of prolonging the life of Peters, and with greater confidence in his own professional judgment than in that of Castleton, omitted the remedies prescribed, it was soon apparent that the deception might prove in vain. I have already intimated that the older physician's perceptions and intuitions were so quick as sometimes to appear almost uncanny; and after asking a question or two, he began to pour upon a square of white paper, from a small vial which he took from one of his vest pockets, a very heavy white powder; and we soon perceived that the powder was to be poured from the paper to the invalid's tongue. Bainbridge was interested in Peters - not only selfishly and with a motive to learn the facts of the old sailor's strange voyage; but he was also interested in the poor old wreck for the sake of the man himself. I saw that in the opinion of Bainbridge, if that white powder were administered to the invalid it would injure him - probably weaken him, and cause a relapse, and perhaps even an earlier death than otherwise might occur; and I saw that Bainbridge was really apprehensive and annoyed. At last he suggested to Castleton to delay the administration of the intended remedy, if only for a few hours. And when Castleton called attention to his own view of the necessity for quick action, involving the instant administration of the dose, it would obviously have been so unwise to contradict him, that Bainbridge did not risk such a course. But, over-anxious to gain his point, he did something still more impolitic. He suggested a remedy of his own by which, he said, Peters would speedily be relieved - a new drug, I believe, or at least a remedy not known to Castleton. For a moment I looked for an explosion of offended dignity; but Castleton controlled his first impulse, and, not looking at Bainbridge, he centred his apparent attention wholly upon myself, and with exceedingly grave vigor, said,

"I, sir, am a member of the Clare County Medical Society - I was once President of that learned body, and have since then for seven consecutive years been its Secretary - my penmanship being illegible to the other members, and often to myself, preventing many disagreements, by precluding a successful reference to the minutes of past meetings. Now, sir, tell me, as man to man, can I consult with, or listen to suggestions - even to suggestions, though worthy of a gigantic intellect - can I listen to suggestions coming from the mentality of a non-member of our learned body? Before replying, let me say that our society is known throughout all of Egypt - that is, you know, Egypt, Illinois. When a medical savant in Paris, or Leipsig, or London, alleges a discovery, we determine the questions of its originality and its value - the chief purpose of our meeting, however, being to present our own discoveries. Now, sir, I appeal to you whether our rules should or should not be strictly obeyed - and the second clause of section three of those rules and regulations - an ethical necessity, and found in the ethical codes of all well-regulated medical societies the world over - says that a member shall not meet in consultation a non-member, even to save a human life - a decidedly remote possibility."

He paused. Neither Bainbridge nor I spoke. In fact, an expression of our thoughts would have been wholly unnecessary, as Castleton appeared to comprehend what was in our minds, as shown by his continued remarks.

"'Liberality,'" you may say: "True, there should be liberality in this eternal world. Individually we *are* liberal - we *are* gentlemen; but it is different with us when you take us as a body. I am for harmony. I admit that at our meetings we do sometimes fight like very devils - life is a conflict, anyway. Sir, the country is full of cursed heresies and growing schisms. - But let me ask - not the doctor here, whom I respect for his immense learning and Cyclopsian (I mean large - not single-eyed) wisdom - what *his* remedy would be? I ask you, sir, not him." Here Doctor Castleton stepped close to my side, and speaking into my ear in a ghastly whisper, said, "The ass isn't Regular!" He then drew back, and looked at me as if expecting astonishment on my part.

I then exchanged a few words with Bainbridge, and informed Castleton of the result. "Ah, ha - ah, ha - indeed," he said, with as near an approach to sarcasm as was possible with him. "So my learned young friend thinks that an organ - the liver -

weighing nearly four pounds is to be moved with a hundredth of a drop of - of - anything! Damn it, sir, am I awake?"

"Ask Doctor Castleton, sir, what portion of a grain of small-pox virus it would require to disseminate over a whole county, if not checked, a dread disease? Ask him from what an oak-tree grows?"

"Ask him," said Castleton, "how long it takes an acorn to act. In this case we require celerity of action - force and penetration."

"Ask him," said Bainbridge, "if the solar rays have celerity, and force, and penetration; and how much they weigh. It requires fine shot to bring down the essence of a disease -"

"Tell him," shouted Castleton, "that the liver is a mammoth that requires a twenty-four-pounder to penetrate its hide. We don't hunt the rhinoceros with bird-shot."

"Say to the gentleman," said Bainbridge, slightly flushed, but still with dignity, "that in this case the animal is not to be slaughtered, but to be cured."

"Damme," said Castleton, "who says slaughtered? - Have I, a surgeon of renown, a gentleman and a scholar, a member of the County Society, sunk so low that I can be called a murderer? Stop - stop where you are - stop in time. Say to the Gentleman that he has gone too far - say that an apology is in order - say that he treads the edge of a living crater. I am dangerous - so my friends say - devilish dangerous" - a smile crossed the face of Bainbridge; and even so slight and transient an appearance as a passing smile was not lost on Castleton, though he seemed to be looking another way - "I mean dangerous on the field of honor. Quackery, sir, is my abhorrence -"

"Come, come, gentlemen," I said, "you are allowing your professional *amour propre* to mislead you. Now," I continued, assuming an air of *bonhomie*, "it seems to me, an outsider, that this whole difference might easily be adjusted. Doctor Castleton here advocates firing twenty-four-pound balls into the patient, and Doctor Bainbridge suggests peppering the invalid with bird-shot. There is certainly room between the bowlders for the bird-shot to slip, and the one will not interfere with the other - I say, give both. Doctor Castleton advises that the dose be immediately given, whilst Doctor Bainbridge appears to think four or five hours hence the better time. I suggest a compromise: let them be given an hour or two hence. There seems to be also some obstacle in the way of one of you giving the other's medicine - so let me administer both the remedies. Now what possible objection can be advanced to this?"

They both laughed; and as Castleton would be on his way home in a few moments, Bainbridge was thoroughly pleased with my proposal. Castleton tacitly consented, and in half a minute seemed to have forgotten the episode - or, at most, gave indication of remembrance only by an apparent desire to be over-agreeable to Bainbridge. A moment later he said to me,

"My dear sir, I hastened my visit here this morning out of consideration for yourself. Last evening after you had departed, Mr. - called at the Loomis House to see you. I happened to meet him as, in some disappointment at having missed you, he was leaving the hotel, where he had learned that you might be gone for two days. I then offered to deliver any message that he should send to you, this morning. When he was informed that you were but ten miles away, in the country, he said that his business with you was pressing; and he asked if it would be possible for you to return to town for a few hours this morning. Then I said that I would convey to you his wishes, and that if you so desired you could be at your hotel before nine o'clock - at which hour he said he would call at the Loomis House, with the hope of meeting you."

I thanked the doctor; and after consulting Bainbridge, said I would avail myself of the offer to return at once to Bellevue. I appreciated that it would be Bainbridge and not I who would have to manage Peters. It was a disappointment to think of missing Peters' story at first-hand; but I hoped to return by the middle of the afternoon, and I knew that Bainbridge could repeat with accuracy all that the old sailor should say. I doubted whether Bainbridge could extract very much from the old man's senile intellect before my return, as the aged voyager was, both in mind and body, quite feeble, and of little endurance. Besides, when once started and warmed to his subject - and very little information could be gained till he was so started - he would no doubt be garrulous.

Doctor Castleton and I started for town at a brisk trot, the doctor having parted from Bainbridge in the best of humors. His last words, shouted back as we drove off, were, "Don't forget the calomel at nine-thirty, doctor; and add to the treatment whatever you may think best. I trust you implicitly. Send me word if you need help."

Strange man! So pleasant, and so harsh; so grand, and so ignoble; so great, and so small; so broad, and so narrow; so kind, and so unkind. As my mind ran along in this channel, I wondered how one and the same man could express the views that he had proclaimed in connection with his medical association, and yet speak of life and death as he had spoken to me on the day preceding. What did he really believe? Could the actor-temperament, displaying itself on most occasions, in connection with a display at times of his natural self, as we say, account for all his eccentricities?

As we fairly flew along the forest road, nearing our destination by a mile in each three minutes, we came to the only hill on the entire route which was considerable, both in extent and in degree of gradient. Doctor Castleton allowed the gait of his horses to slacken into a slow walk; and - ever nervous, ever active - he reached into the side pocket of his linen duster, and drew forth a small book, apparently fresh from the publisher.

"'The Mistakes of the Gods, and Other Lectures,'" he said,

looking at the back of the volume, and reading its title. "Ah, 'The Gods.' The title, sir, almost tells the whole story; and so far as you and I are concerned, it is almost a waste of time for us to open the book - and a crime against themselves for ignorant men to do so."

"The author must be one of your 'holy terrors' that I hear mentioned," I said. "A Western 'bad man' no doubt. Sad! sad! is it not?"

"Oh, no, no; the author is not a cowboy - he's a perfect gentleman - as polished as I am; and there's nothing very sad in the book. It contains several lectures in the line of agnostic agitation, which were from time to time delivered by a very talented, but, as I think, mistaken man. When I say mistaken, I do not mean mistaken in the sense that our church people might apply the term to him; for our church people seem to misunderstand him, almost as greatly as he misapprehends the purposes of nineteenth-century Anglo-Saxon Christian workers. But mark my words, sir, you will soon, in England, hear of this young 'infidel' lecturer; for with his keen brain, his invincible logic, his concise and beautiful rhetoric, he will soon be recognized as the most popular living agnostic. His home is not far distant from Bellevue, and I have frequently heard him lecture. I think him the best platform orator I have ever listened to, though I have twice been charmed by the eloquence of Phillips, and a dozen times by that of Beecher. I shall not outrage your own and my own manhood by alluding to anything which the more partisan church people say of this brilliant agnostic; and I say what I do, only because in your distant home you may some day wonder just what is behind an agnostic demonstration such as he is leading up to, and which is certain to centralize the dissatisfied spirit of the country into an anti-church propaganda of no mean proportions. I am opposed to such a movement; but I believe in truth as the only durable weapon, and I love truth for truth's sake - I should refuse to enter the gateway of heaven if liars were admitted. I cannot go into the history of this man, but this much is fact: There are reasons which cause him to believe that in striking at

Christianity he is performing a highly praiseworthy action. In this belief he is as sincere and as enthusiastic in his cold logical way, as is any Christian in *his* belief. If duplicity were possible to this man - or if he could have found it consistent with his sense of right even to keep silence concerning his opinion on religious subjects - he would by this time have been Governor of Illinois; and, with his ability, there is no elective office in the country to which he might not aspire with reasonable certainty of success. He himself is aware of all this, as are all who know him. At the early age of thirty-three, before his views were generally known, he was our Attorney-General. No political party will ever again dare to nominate him for an office."

"This is all wrong," I said; "it savors of religious persecution."

"True," said Castleton, "it does; but the fact is as I state it. He would if he ran for office lose enough votes from his own party to allow his opponent to win."

"But, my dear doctor," I said, "I fail to catch your reasons for thinking this man mistaken. You surely would not have him be untrue to himself?"

"Oh, no - never that! I mean that he is intellectually mistaken in thinking that the world is still to be benefited by agnostic agitation among the masses. Voltaire had a good reason for proclaiming and teaching his views, because in France, in his day, religious infidelity was necessary to political liberty. Tom Paine had a good reason for his course, because Christianity, misrepresented at that time by mistaken or corrupt men, was arrayed on the side of the despot, and so continued up to the beginning of the French Revolution. But this man has no good excuse for a fight against church influence in the United States, now in 1877. The influence of the Christian church is now certainly exerted for good, and does not attempt to restrict the liberty of any man, or of society."

"But did you not just say that this agnostic's views would forever prevent his election to public office, here in this great free country, in the year 1877 and onward?"

"We cannot have a free country and not allow a man to vote against another, even if his vote were influenced by the cut of a candidate's trousers."

"Yes," I said; "but if the cut of a candidate's trousers influenced a man's vote, such a man would be a good object for education. Your agnostic would no doubt say that the influence of church is to be fought so long as it judges of a man's capability to do one thing well by his opinion on a totally different subject."

"You will never educate the people out of their prejudices; but I myself should vote against this man because his course shows his views to be inconsistent with statesmanship. No person desires to restrict another's individual opinions; we only combat this man's because of their effects, as he combats those of his opponents. There are as many agnostics, proportionally, that would not vote for a Presbyterian, for instance, for public office, as there are Presbyterians who, under like circumstances, would not vote for an agnostic."

"But in what way does the belief, or want of belief, of an agnostic, prevent an otherwise able man from being a statesman?" I asked.

"No doubt some of the best statesmen living are agnostics; but they are not agnostic agitators. Men who are able to digest and assimilate agnostic opinions, are able to initiate those ideas for themselves; and only men who are able to properly digest and assimilate such ideas should have them at all."

"Can you," I asked, "state an instance in which what you indicate as premature education of the masses in agnostic ideas, might lead to injury to the persons so instructed, or to society at large?"

"Yes, sir, I can. Your ignorant American - the 'cracker' element of the South, your ignorant Italian, and your ignorant Irishman are injured by taking away their religious beliefs. The first of these, when church people, dress neatly, are honorable, and have some upward-tending ambitions; whilst those of them that are infidels are reduced - men and women - to a state of ambitionless inertia and tobacco saturation - if no worse. The two latter are either under religious control, or under secret-society control. If the lower-class Irishman or Italian, unendowed with judgment to rightly use the little knowledge he already possesses - to properly interpret his own feelings or guide his own impulses - has not his church with its priestly control, he will have his secret-society with its secret executive control, its bovine fury, and its senseless pertinacity, the poison-bowl and the dagger. For my part, if a man must either seek liberty from ambush, and learn independence through treachery, or else be on his knees before a graven image, suited to his mental calibre - let us keep him on his knees till he can rise to something better than murder. Why, sir, an Irish Republican (a rarity) - an editor, once said to me that some of our Irish emigrants have hair on their teeth when they get to America; and, though I may be wrong, I never see an Italian organ-grinder without first thinking of a dagger between my ribs, and then settling down to a comfortable feeling that if the fellow's a Catholic the confessional stands between me and such a danger. The man who attempts to teach such fellows about complete liberty should be responsible for any consequent acts."

"Still, doctor," I said, "the road to universal knowledge cannot be all smooth. Ground must be broken by somebody. If there is anything in Christianity that bars the way to final freedom of mind for the whole human race, then I myself say, clear away the obstructions - the work cannot begin too soon or continue too vigorously."

"I see nothing in true Christianity but good for the human race - surely you speak only to call out my own views. If there is anything in any church policy or polity which requires reforming, let it be reformed."

"Excuse me, doctor," I said; "but I had thought you yourself an agnostic. Do you not think that if a religion will not bear the test of cold reason, it should be discarded from the lives of men?"

"No, I do not. The human mind is not comprised in intellect alone - it has its moral or emotional side, wholly apart from reason. Religion is not to be reasoned about - it is to be felt. No founder of a religion ever claimed for it a place in man's reason. Now just think for a minute. Let us leave the ignorant, and consider what the best of men are - men who have attained a mental cultivation certainly as great as will ever be possible to the masses. Take the very highest society in England and America - to what extent are its members controlled by *reason,* and to what extent by *feeling* and by the fixed sentiments growing out of feeling? Ratiocination does not influence one of their actions in a million. There is not within my knowledge a single instance where a purely rational conception has been the basis of practice, in opposition to feeling."

"Surely," I said, "you do not mean to say that educated men are not governed in the main by reason?"

"I mean just what I say - that I do not know, in practice, a single instance in which they are so governed in opposition to feeling. Pshaw, pshaw young man; if we are to compel the acts of practical daily life to conform with a dialectic demonstration of what is best for us - to do only what is in reason best for us - we must simply cease to live, though we do continue to breathe. Even in physics, of what use are logical demonstrations, when the premises are only a foundation more unstable than quicksand - purely provisional?

"Now if these agnostics were truthful - which they try to be; and were consistent - which they are not, they would be in a trying situation. Reason shows no advantage to a man in kissing his wife; he has no syllogistic endorsement for supporting her and the children; in fact, he has no business to have children - all the result of feeling or sentiment, all rubbish, and beneath the intellect of a man who worships Pure Reason! And if the demands of man's moral or affectional nature are a reason for such indulgences, then his aspirations to the great primal cause of the known, the unknown, and (to us here and now) unknowable wonders and mysteries of the universe without, and of ourselves within, is also justifiable in reason, and ought not by wit and eloquence to be juggled out of the ingenuous mind. The masses are governed by religion, directly and indirectly, to an extent much greater than at first thought appears. The daily life of the agnostic himself is shaped by his Christian heredity and environment. Now our Author furnishes no substitute for this intuitive demand of being. If reason can supply nothing in place of religion, why not allow those who possess religious conviction to retain so agreeable, and to others beneficial, a belief? - Now right here I can detect the voice of the agnostic agitator - this is his strongest situation, and he simply smiles when you make this opening for him. The voice says, 'Agreeable? Agreeable to burn forever in hell? Well, well, my friend - our ideas of pleasure differ.' This is sophistical twaddle. It is not the Christian that suffers from a fear of hell - it is the sinner, through his guilty conscience. Conscience, conscience; the only barrier between us and hell on earth! Christians are comforted by the thought of a loving Christ - Christians, in my experience, do not suffer."

"Why, sir," I said, "I cannot but wonder that you are not yourself a professed Christian."

"Never mind me, young man. - But here we are on the edge of town. I could, if I wanted to, preach a sermon capable of converting every heathen within sound of my voice. Once, at a camp-meeting, I did preach a sermon; and I tell you, the old people looked mighty sober, and the younger and more susceptible of my auditors covered their faces with their hands and seemed to shake with grief and contrition. But, pshaw, pshaw; people don't go to hear either witty agnostics lecture, or preachers preach, to get something for their brain-boxes to reason about. Believe me " - tapping the volume, still in his hand - "this sort of thing won't make anybody reason. After all, the question is one of swapping off Christ for an Illinois lawyer."

THE EIGHTH CHAPTER

It lacked half an hour of nine o'clock as we drove up before the Loomis House, where I alighted, and ran up to my rooms. I had scarcely more than made a hasty toilet, when Arthur came in. After telling me who had, during my absence, called to see me, and after attending to some trifling wants which I expressed, he shuffled his feet in a style that I had learned to recognize as indicating a desire to say something not within the compass of our purely business relationship - a liberty which the precedents of our first two days of acquaintanceship in connection with later events had solidified into a vested right.

"Well, Arthur?" I said.

"I read the whole book, sir - there it is, on the table. That book just did get me. But what did become of Pym and Peters? And is it true you've found that old soc-doligin' pirate?"

I told him that Peters was found.

"Well, now!" he continued. "I'd like to see the old four-foot-eighter. But if you love me, tell me what that white curtain reachin' down from the sky was, and what made the ocean bilin' hot? What made them ante-artic niggers so 'fraid of everything white, and what was the hiryglificks on the black marble meant to say? And, most of all, who was the female that stood in the way of the boat? Say - I don't blame anybody - but if Mr. Poe knowed he didn't know these points, what did he get our mouths waterin' for? Did you find out these points yet?"

I explained to him that probably at that very moment Doctor Bainbridge was sitting on the edge of Dirk Peters' cot, drinking in the wonderful story; and that as soon as a certain gentleman had called to see me, I expected to return to Peters' house, and to remain until we knew all.

"Go slow," said Arthur, "and don't fall down on any importing points. Better take time, and catch everything. I asked Doctor Castleton last night what made that ocean bile; and he said he guessed the mouth of hell was down that way, and Satin had just opened the door to air out. That's him; if it ain't heaven it's got to be hell. But how old Peters ever lived this long with Castleton monkeyin' with him is a mighty funny thing. - But who's that?"

A rap had sounded on my door. My caller had arrived.

I did not succeed in getting back to Bainbridge and Peters so soon as I had expected. My business in the town dragged along far into the evening, and it was nine o'clock by the time I was at liberty. At ten o'clock I sent for a conveyance, and was driven to Peters' house, where I arrived just before midnight.

I found Peters sleeping soundly, and Bainbridge dozing in a chair. My entrance aroused Bainbridge. He arose, smiling, and was apparently glad to see me. I saw at a glance that he had been successful in obtaining from Peters the secrets of his antarctic voyage. "Well?" I asked.

"The information which I have gained," said Bainbridge, "even could I procure no more, would suffice to explain all those mysteries that Poe hints at as fact, and much that he seems to apprehend with that sixth sense which in the genius approaches a union of clairvoyance and prescience - mysteries of which he does not speak in language sufficiently clear for common comprehension. At all events, I am not disappointed; and more may yet be procured. There remains much of interest, in the way of *minutiae*, which I expect to learn to-morrow. I know now what made that antarctic region more than tropical, and what the white curtain was - and is. I know how the hieroglyphics came in the caverns of black marl. That antarctic country exceeds, in the truly wonderful, anything in the world, old or new, with which I am acquainted, or of which I have heard."

"But is it true? Have you not been listening to fairy tales? - or, rather, to sailor tales?"

"When to-morrow I tell you what I have, hour after hour, with brief rests, drawn from that poor old battered hulk" - he pointed toward Peters' cot - "and when you consider what he is - then say if he is the man, or his sailor friends are the men, to invent such a story. I admit that at times during the day his mind seemed to wander slightly, and that he has the usual faculty of sea-faring men for exaggeration; so that at times I had to employ my best discrimination to enable me to separate the real from the fanciful, that I might retain the true and discard the untrue. He seems to have lived for more than a year in proximity to the South Pole, and his experiences were as marvellous as that country is strangely grand, and its people truly wonderful - Oh, no - nothing on the Gulliver order; the people are not dwarfs or giants, and they have no horses either that talk or that do not talk; no yahoos - nothing in that line. 'Wings?' Oh, no - no flying men or women, no women in gauze, either; everything quite in good taste and genteel. Just wait, now; you'll hear it all in an orderly way - which I myself did not, however. 'One-eyed?' I told you, just now, that it was all in good taste and genteel. No, no; nothing Homeric - no sheep, and no sirens. Now, I'm really tired, and you'll not succeed in starting me on a story that'll take six or eight hours to tell, even if we do not stop to discuss matters as we progress. To-morrow, as I before said, we will get from Peters all other possible facts, and no doubt we shall gather further particulars; then we will go to town. I intend to come out here every day till Peters gets better or dies - and I suppose you will not refuse to keep me company. Every evening we will meet in my rooms, or in yours, and I will recite the story in my own way. Now does that satisfy you?"

It satisfied me fully, I said; and then we spread our blankets, and made a night of it on the floor.

The next day Bainbridge spent the forenoon, for the most part, sitting on the edge of Dirk Peters' cot, listening to the old man talk, describe, explain. I walked out, and explored the immediately adjacent country, entertaining myself as best I could. At about two o'clock in the afternoon we started for town, leaving Peters much better than when two days before we had first, together, entered his humble home. We promised to see him the next day; and, in fact, one or both of us returned each day for many succeeding days. That evening Doctor Bainbridge came to my rooms, and began the recitation of Dirk Peters' story; and that, too, was continued from day to day.

And it is now time that the patient reader should also know the secrets of that far-distant antarctic region - secrets of which Poe himself died in ignorance - save as the genius, the seer, knows the wonders of heaven and earth - sees gems that lie in hidden places, and flowers that bloom obscurely, and feels the mysteries of ocean depths, and all that is so far - or near, so great - or small, that common vision sees it not.

THE NINTH CHAPTER

There may be among my readers some who have never read "The Narrative of A. Gordon Pym," or have so long ago perused that interesting and mysterious conception, that they have forgotten even the outlines of the story. It is the purpose of the present chapter to review a few of the incidents in that narrative, a knowledge of which will add to the clearer understanding of Peters' story.

Those who are familiar with Edgar Allan Poe's admirable and entrancing narrative just mentioned, are aware that it is written in autobiographical form, the facts for the most part being furnished by Pym in the shape of journal or diary entries, which are edited by Mr. Poe. For such readers it will be but a waste of time to peruse the present chapter, brief though it is. And let me further say to any chance reader of mine who has never had opportunity to enjoy that exciting and edifying work of America's great genius of prose fiction, that he is to be envied the possession of the belated pleasure that awaits him - only a treasured memory of which delight remains to the rest of us.

From my own narrative I shall omit much of description and colloquy which, during its development in 1877, occurred concerning discoveries of a geographical and geological nature, and also many discussions of a character purely philosophical; but no fact shall be discarded. The historian has, in my opinion, no discretionary power concerning the introduction or elimination of facts. His duty is plain, and in the present instance it shall be faithfully performed.

The following presents a very general outline of "The Narrative of A. Gordon Pym":

In the year 1827, Pym, just verging upon manhood, runs away from his home in the town of Nantucket, on the island of the same name, in companionship with his boy friend, Augustus Barnard, son of the captain of the ship on which they depart. The name of the brig on which they embark is the Grampus, which is starting for a trading voyage in the South Pacific Ocean. Young Barnard secretes Pym in the hold of the brig, to remain hidden until so far from land as to make a return of the runaway impracticable. Pym, hidden amid the freightage of the hold, falls into a prolonged slumber, probably caused by the foul air in that part of the vessel. When the brig is four days at sea, a majority of the crew mutiny; and after killing many of those who have not joined them, Captain Barnard is set adrift in a small boat, without food and with only a jug of water. Young Barnard is permitted to remain on the vessel. There is a dog that plays a leading part in the mutiny episode by acting as a messenger between Barnard and Pym, who had no other means of communicating.

Next comes a counter mutiny, made necessary to preserve the life of one Peters, a sailor to whom Barnard owes his life. The ship's cook is determined to kill Peters, and is about to accomplish his purpose, when Peters, young Barnard, and a sailor named Parker, who joins the two, devise a plan for overcoming the mutineers of the "cook's party." This they succeeded in doing by, at the right moment, producing from his hiding-place young Pym, who is dressed to resemble a certain murdered sailor whose corpse is still on the brig; and during the fright of the "cook's party," Peters and Parker kill the cook and his followers.

Then the four - Barnard, Pym, Peters, and the sailor Parker - have many thrilling adventures. The brig is finally wrecked in a storm, and only the inverted hull remains above water, to which the four cling for many days. The party is at last rescued by a trading-vessel on its way to discover new lands in the Antarctic Ocean. They reach 83 south latitude, soon after which a landing is made on an island inhabited by a tribe of strange black people. Here, through a trick of the islanders, the crew lose their lives - all save Pym and Peters. Parker had already died, and in a manner more entertaining to the reader in the perusal than to Parker in the performance; and which, Peters said forty-nine years later, the mere thought of, always made him willing to wait for his supper when he had of necessity to forego a dinner.

Whilst escaping in a small boat from this island, Pym and Peters abduct one of the male natives. Like his fellows, this native is black, even to his teeth; in fact, there is nothing white on the whole island; even the water has its peculiarities. And also like his fellows, he dreads the color *white*; and whenever he sees anything white he becomes almost frenzied or paralyzed with terror. The small boat with its three occupants is carried on an ocean current, to the south. One day Pym, in taking a white handkerchief from his pocket allows the wind to flare it into the face of the black islander, who sinks in convulsions to the bottom of the boat, later moaning (as had moaned the other islanders on seeing white), "Tekeli-li, tekeli-li." He continued to breathe, and no more. The following day the body of a white animal floats by, a body similar to one which they had seen on the beach of the island last visited. Then they see in the south a white curtain, which, after their further progress in its direction, they observe reaches from the sky to the water. The water of the ocean current which is hurrying them along becomes hour by hour warmer, and finally hot. An ash-like material, which seems to melt as it touches the water, falls all around and over them. Gigantic white birds fly from beyond the white curtain, screaming the eternal "Teke-li-li, tekeli-li" - a syllabication that dies away on the lips of the islander as his soul finally, on that last terrible day, leaves his body.

The last words of the last of Pym's entries in his journal are

Charles Romyn Dake

as follows:

"And now we rushed into the embraces of the cataract, where a chasm threw itself open to receive us. But there arose in our pathway a shrouded human figure, very far larger in its proportions than any dweller among men. And the hue of the skin of the figure was of the perfect whiteness of the snow."

The following description of Dirk Peters as he appeared in the year 1827, or just fifty years before I saw him, apparently a man of seventy-five years (though we finally concluded that he was nearer eighty), is Pym's, quoted from Poe's narrative:

"This man was the son of an Indian woman of the tribe of Upsarokas, who live among fastnesses of the Black Hills, near the source of the Missouri. His father was a fur-trader, I believe, or at least connected in some manner with the Indian trading-posts on Lewis River. Peters himself was one of the most ferocious looking men I ever beheld. He was short in stature, not more than four feet eight inches high, but his limbs were of Herculean mould. His hands, especially, were so enormously thick and broad as hardly to retain a human shape. His arms, as well as his legs, were bowed in the most singular manner, and appeared to possess no flexibility whatever. His head was equally deformed, being of immense size, with an indentation on the crown (like that on the head of most negroes) and entirely bald. To conceal this latter deficiency, which did not proceed from old age, he usually wore a wig formed of any hair-like material which presented itself - occasionally the skin of a Spanish dog or American grizzly bear. At the time spoken of, he had on a portion of one of these bear-skins; and it added no little to the natural ferocity of his countenance, which betook of the Upsaroka character. The mouth extended nearly from ear to ear; the lips were thin, and seemed, like some other portions of his frame, to be devoid of natural pliancy, so that the ruling expression never varied under the influence of any emotion whatever. This ruling expression may be conceived when it is considered that the teeth were exceedingly long and protruding, and were never even partially covered, in any instance, by the lips. To pass this man with a casual glance, one might imagine him to be convulsed with laughter; but a second look would induce a shuddering acknowledgment, that if such an expression were indicative of merriment, the merriment must be that of a demon. Of this singular being many anecdotes were prevalent among the seafaring men of Nantucket. These anecdotes went to prove his prodigious strength when under excitement, and some of them had given rise to a doubt of his sanity."

THE TENTH CHAPTER

During the early evening of the day on which Doctor Bainbridge and I returned from our stay with Dirk Peters, I sat in my room at the Loomis House, impatiently awaiting the moment when Bainbridge was to arrive. I knew that he was wearied by his labors with Peters, and I did not anticipate a prolonged talk from him. Still, I was anxious to hear at least a beginning of the promised story. At the appointed time he came in, and placing a roll of paper on the table, took the large easy-chair which I had placed for him.

"As I know," he said, "that the developments of the past three days must, quite naturally, have developed a curiosity in you of some intensity to hear the sequel of the Pym adventures, I shall endeavor not to keep you unnecessarily waiting; but shall allay at once a portion of your curiosity. Later - tomorrow, if agreeable - I will deal with the particulars of that strange voyage - perhaps the strangest ever made by man."

He picked up, and smoothed out upon the table, the roll of paper which he had brought with him; and then continued:

"In the first place, I will briefly and in a very general way describe for you the south polar region, which, I feel certain, Pym and Peters reached, and where they resided for somewhat more than one year. Here is a map which I have with some care drawn from rough sketches jotted down as I sat on the edge of Peters' cot, and each of which sketches I had him verify.

A. Central space of boiling lava Diameter 15 miles. Probable situation South Pole

B. Ring of hot lava, white hot at inner edge, red hot at outer edge. Width, about 4 miles

C. Ring of hot lava, dull red, shading to black heat at outer edge. Width, about 4 miles

D. Ring 4m in width. Blocks of lava, rock salt, and coral-like terrains

EEE. Volcanic mountains, up to 8m in height and valleys

FFF. Antarctic Ocean with islands

SOUTH POLAR REGION *and* HILI-LI LAND.

"Now move this way with your chair, and look at this map. And in the first place, I will tell you that at the South Pole - probably not precisely at the pole, but certainly within the sixth of a degree of it - is a circular surface of absolutely white-hot, boiling lava, about fifteen miles in diameter. This surface was, in ages past, as indicated by surroundings, many times its present surface extent - say from seventy to seventy-five miles across. No doubt the surface of the earth at the Antarctic Pole had once cooled, and later become covered with water, though with very shallow water - probably at some points by none, at others by a depth of ten or fifteen feet. From some cause - and many causes might be imagined - this earth-and-water surface of say two hundred miles in circumference, sank into the interior of the earth, and the boiling lava came to the surface. We can scarcely conceive of the awful effect when the Antarctic Sea poured over the circumference of this mass of boiling earth and metal.

"Now it must be considered that this boiling lava was not merely a great surface of white-hot matter, in which case it would, relatively speaking, soon have cooled. To flood its edges with an overflow of ten feet of water would be comparable to running a film of water a hundredth of an inch in depth over the top of a red-hot stove in which a large fire continues to burn and constantly to renew the heat on its surface. This surface of boiling lava must have had a practically limitless depth, and the water which poured over it must have evaporated instantly. After thinking the matter over, with the *data* which I have well in view, I concluded that it required about two hundred years for the water to reach the limit which it finally attained as water *en masse*. A little thought on the subject has shown me that Peters is telling the truth, because his description, to my mind, harmonizes with the laws of physics. One of the earliest phenomena presented by this condition, was that so much sea-water evaporated, and evaporated so rapidly, that masses of rock-salt formed, creating a partial barrier to the inroads of the sea - I say a partial barrier, because the deliquescence of salt would cause it to be the poorest of all barriers to water. Still, we must remember that the immediately surrounding water must have reached, so far as salt is concerned, the saturation point, and would have been a very slow solvent of hard rock-salt in enormous masses and several miles in extent. Then, two other conditions soon arose: First, the warm surrounding water permitted a coral-like development, as shown by present appearances, and second, volcanic action began.

"Now look at my map. This inner circle represents the present area of boiling lava, which, as I have said, is about fifteen miles in diameter - the South Pole, according to the natives, being at about the point corresponding to this dot, marked 'a.' The ring next without the circle I have made to represent a zone of lava which is at its inner edge white-hot, and at its outer edge red-hot, its width, let us say, as the division is arbitrary, about four miles. The second circle represents a zone of lava which is dull red at its inner edge, and black, but hot, at its outer. Of course the lava blends away from white-hot within, to barely warm without; but I thus map it, the better to picture reigning conditions. The next circle, some four or five miles in width, represents a ring of cold lava-blocks, masses of rock-salt, and animalculine remains, from twenty-five to two hundred feet high. Outside of this last-mentioned zone, we have several rings of volcanic mountains with intervening valleys, and many active craters at the summit of mountains; while on the mountain-sides lie numerous masses of rock-salt, thrown from below by eruptive action, glistening in the brilliant volcanic light, and slowly deliquescing. This zone of mountains and valleys is from ten to twenty miles in width, and whilst in the main its mountains are not more than from half a mile to a mile high, it contains peaks of five or six miles in height, and there is one peak which rises nine miles above the sea-level.

"I want you to look particularly at these larger mountain-ranges, one at the right, the other at the left side of my map - each of which as it stretches out into the sea divides into two smaller chains. Upon these ranges, and the comparatively diminutive height of the intervening mountains, in connection with the fact that there is a constant wind-current from the lower Pacific (generally speaking, from the west of longitude 74 W.), depends the habitability of this large island, the Island of Hili-li (here represented in about longitude 75 E.), and many other islands which stretch out in the same direction from this enormous active surface-crater. I say that upon such conditions depends the habitability of these islands, and so I believe; but there is another cause for their greater than tropical warmth: If you will glance here on the right of this map, in the midst of the mountain zone you will see represented a bay, which, winding among mountains, makes its way very close to the zone of hot lava - in fact, is divided from it by little more than the ring of lava-blocks, rock-salt, and animal remains, which at this point is narrowed to a width of about two miles. The temperature of the water of this bay at its inner extremity is probably about 180 F. - say 32 below the boiling-point of distilled water; and it flows in a steady current past the Island of Hili-li. This bay is undoubtedly fed from the opposite side of the great crater, and its supply flows for miles in contact with hot lava. It is probable that this extremely warm water current greatly assists the hot-air current in creating the super-tropical climate of Hili-li.

"And now, as I have in part satisfied your curiosity, and as I am somewhat exhausted with my two days' and nights' experience with Peters, I know you will permit me to rest at so suitable a stopping-point. To-morrow evening I will take up the story of Dirk Peters where it joins the sudden break in Pym's journal, and will carry you along to the time when the inhabitants of Hili-li thought that the atmosphere of some other land would be more conducive to Peters' longevity and health, as well as to their own tranquillity. And I assure your Sultanship, that the story I shall relate to you to-morrow night will be more interesting than the dry physical facts which I have this evening imparted, and which it seemed best that you should know before hearing in consecutive detail the particulars of Peters' voyage."

I assented to his suggestions, thanking him for the clear description which he had given of that strange region, and for the pains he had taken to draft of it so accurate a map - which map he allowed me to retain. I was about to ask a question, when the door opened, and Doctor Castleton rushed into the room.

"Well, how's the old man?" he asked.

We described Peters' condition; and I even recounted a few of the facts which Bainbridge had just imparted to me. Then I asked the question which Castleton's abrupt entry had delayed.

"But," I asked, "has not Peters' imagination, owing to the administration of drugs, been unnaturally stimulated? There are drugs which it is commonly believed may have a wonderful effect in stimulating the imagination to flights of marvellous grandeur."

"No," said Bainbridge. "The doctor here will say the same. No drug on earth could produce even an approach to such an effect."

"Certainly not," said Castleton. "The mass of laymen are not only ignorant - excuse me, sir, but I know you want the facts - not only ignorant, but extremely and persistently ignorant on this subject. I have heard it said that Byron drank twelve - or perhaps twenty - bottles of wine the night he wrote 'The

Corsair.' If he did, he simply wrote 'The Corsair' in spite of the wine. I have heard it stated that Poe was intoxicated when he wrote 'The Raven' - which is not only an untrue statement but one that could not possibly be true, and which certainly every man who ever attempted to write under the influence of an alcoholic stimulant knows to be false. Drugs - including alcohol - which are supposed to stimulate what we might term a rational imagination, only stimulate an irrational fancy. They seem to the person affected to cause a play of imagination, but they really produce only a state of nervous action which causes their subject to feel appreciation of otherwise trifling mental pictures that in themselves are flimsy nothings. Let a man so affected try to impart to another his fancies, and - well, who has not been bored by a drunken man? Did De Quincey, with that superb mind, succeed in fancying anything that even he could tell? He speaks of glowing drug-born fancies, but he describes nothings. Now Milton, the old Puritan - the cold-water man - he had fancies which he was able to transmit, and which are worthy to be forever treasured. The early Greeks were exceedingly temperate, and the men who composed the 'Nostoi' were not drunkards - Homer sang the 'Iliad' and the 'Odyssey' with a sober tongue, and a sober brain back of his utterances. The man who gets drunk to write poetry, will find it easier to write his poetry on the following morning, spite of headache, blue-devils, and all." He paused for a moment; and then this peculiar man continued:

"And I know! Why, sir, I have drunk barrels of whiskey - barrels of the stuff. I have seen whiskey-snakes in squirming masses three feet deep. I have gone into a parlor, and had a lady say when she saw me fumbling in my pockets: 'Doctor, your handkerchief is in your back pocket.' Bless her! I was only putting back into my pockets the jim-jam snake-heads as the snakes *would* try to emerge! I pity a weak devil that goes home and to bed because of a mild attack of delirium tremens. I brush the vipers away with a sweep of my hand, and go about my business. But I myself draw the line at roosters. A man who may laugh at snakes will quail before roosters. A fellow may shut his eyes to snakes, but he can't shut his ears to roosters.

Charles Romyn Dake

Well, well: it's all in a life-time. But, believe me, no good poetry, either in verse or in prose, is drunkenman poetry."

With which final remark he shot out of the room. Then Doctor Bainbridge took his departure, and I retired to sleep and to dream of fiery craters, with snakes crawling out of them, and gigantic roosters picking up the snakes one by one and dropping them over a mountain of salt into a lake of boiling water. I was pleased when morning came, and I heard the comparatively cheering tinkle from bells on the team of mules drawing the little "bob-tail" street-car past the hotel.

THE ELEVENTH CHAPTER

On the following evening Bainbridge came to my room as he had promised, arriving at about eight o'clock. I had not that day accompanied him on his visit to Peters, who it seems was daily gaining strength. I had spent my day in reading, except that Arthur had repeatedly come to my room, remaining for fifteen or twenty minutes at a time as his duties would permit, being curious to learn from me "some of the things about that ante-arctic country," etc. He was much interested in the subject, and studied with close attention the map made by Doctor Bainbridge. Arthur had asked permission to be present when the doctor should come in the evening, but I thought better to deny him that privilege. Doctor Bainbridge was taking the matter seriously, and I knew Arthur too well to expect from him a decorous reticence at any time. I could imagine the effect on Bainbridge as he closed some glowing description, should Arthur jump up with a remark about "ante-arctic niggers," or "gee whallopin big females." I had occasion later to know that my caution was most judicious, and to condemn myself for a want of firmness in maintaining so sensible a decision.

Doctor Bainbridge, without unnecessary delay or preliminary remark, began the relation of Peters' adventures at the point indicated by him the evening before as the proper place of commencement.

"The great white curtain you have no doubt already surmised to be a clear-cut line of dense fog, due to the fact that a

Charles Romyn Dake

perpendicular plane of extremely cold air in that situation cuts through an atmosphere which, on both sides of this sheet of frigid air, is exceedingly warm, and laden with moisture to the saturation-point. This curtain of fog is so thin that sudden gusts of wind, upon either of its surfaces, drive it aside much as a double curtain is thrown on either side by the arms of a person passing between. It was through such an opening that Pym and Peters rushed, on a cross-current of warm water which was carrying them along. The figure of a large, pure-white woman, into whose arms their half-delirious fancies pictured them as rushing, was simply a large statue of spotless marble, which stands at the entrance of the bay of Hili-li. The ash-like material which for days had rained upon them and into the ocean around them, was no longer seen. It proved to have been a peculiar volcano dust or crater ash, which, carried into the upper air, fell at a distance - sometimes directly on Hili-li; but rarely so close as within eighty or ninety miles of the central fire.

"They had scarcely passed the white fog-curtain when they were accosted by a gay party of young men and young women, numbering some eight or ten persons, in an elegant pleasure-boat. Pym and Peters being ignorant of the language of Hili-li land, and the Hili-lites being ignorant of the English tongue, it was of course impossible for them to hold converse beyond that permitted by signs. The pleasure party, however, saw at once that the two men were almost ready to expire from want of food and rest. The Hili-lites took them into their own spacious boat, and hastened to a landing-place in the suburbs of the capital and metropolis of the nation, Hili-li City. There they all disembarked, and the strangers were supported across a lawn, the grass of which was of the palest green - (so nearly white, in fact, that its greenness of tint would scarcely have been noticed but for the contrast afforded by many brilliant white flowers that appeared here and there amid the grass) - up to a palace, the equal of which, for size and beauty, neither of the Americans had before seen, though Pym was familiar with the external appearance of the finest residences in and about Boston, and also of those on the Hudson River just above New

York; whilst Peters had been in most of the sea-coast cities of the habitable world.

"They were taken into this palace, were immediately escorted to the bath (which Peters declined to enter), were furnished with liquid nourishments, and were then allowed to sleep - which both of them did, uninterruptedly, for twenty-four hours. When they awoke they were furnished with new clothing of the best (the Hili-lites dressed something in the style of Louis XIV.), and then invited to a full repast. So well were they treated that in less than a week they felt quite as strong and otherwise natural as they had on leaving the harbor of Nantucket.

"So elegant and expressive, yet so simple was the language of Hili-li, that Pym could in two weeks understand and speak it sufficiently well for ordinary converse; whilst Peters was able to employ it sufficiently for his purposes, in about a month.

"The residents of the palace seemed to comprehend just about what had happened to the strangers. It appears that once or twice in a century strangers similar in general exterior to this pair had arrived in that region, generally in small boats, and on one occasion in a ship; but none of the strangers had desired to depart from a land so beautiful, to undertake a voyage both long and hazardous - none save the persons who had come in a ship nearly three centuries before - (you will recall what I told you of the small book that I read in the Astor Library). As there was little which the Hili-lites had any desire to learn from the strangers, there was not much to be said, anyway. Pym and Peters were permitted to roam at will, and many Hili-lites came to look at them. The palace in which they were permitted to reside belonged to a cousin of the king, so that no troublesome surveillance was inflicted upon these wrecked sailors - in fact, so completely isolated were the two, that no feelings except a mild degree of sympathy and curiosity were excited by their presence on the island. A small boat was at their disposal, and they soon almost daily took the liberty of rowing across the harbor to the wharf at the end of the main street of Hili-li, where they would disembark, and wander for hours around this strange old city, viewing in wonderment its beauties, its peculiarities, its mysteries.

"Hili-li is a city of from one to two hundred thousand people. But, oh, lovely beyond power of language to describe! - past all conception, and comparable alone with fancies such as float through the brain of poet-lover as he lies dreaming of his soul's desire. I draw my conclusions from Peters' state of mind when he attempts to describe this strange city, rather than from what he says; and also from some of Pym's remarks on the subject, which Peters was able to repeat. In your imagination, compass within an area two miles in diameter the choicest beauties of ancient Greece and Egypt, Rome and Persia; then brighten them with natural surrounding scenery such as Homer and Dante and Milton might have dreamed of - and you may feel a little of what Pym and Peters felt when first they saw this glorious island. In ancient Greece a true democrat would have been displeased with the extreme discrepancy between the grandeur of public buildings, and the poverty of private dwellings; but in Hili-li these two bore a perfectly just relationship of elegance, each in its way being perfect.

"Yet mere inanimate beauties were the least of all. Even Peters, old and dying - never a man to whom art spoke in more than whispers - even he was aroused from the arms of death when he spoke of the women of Hili-li. 'Were they blondes?' I asked him. 'No.' 'Were they brunettes?' 'No.' They were simply entrancing - never to be forgotten. Each and everyone of them, like Helen, won by her mere presence the adoration of man. And the men - even they must have been superb - were types of perfect manly elegance.

"I spent many hours in trying to draw from Peters facts which I might put together and so become competent to explain the perfection, physical and mental - for they possessed both of these charms - of the Hili-lites. And after combining what Peters could describe, and what he could recall of Pym's sayings, with a statement or two of the natives that clings in the old man's memory, I formed what I am able to assure you is a reliable opinion of the origin of the Hili-lite race:

"At about the most trying period of the barbarian invasion of Southern Europe - certainly preceding the foundation of Venice, and I think in the fourth century - when the enlightened peoples of the Mediterranean were fleeing hither and thither like rats in a burning house from which but few escape - during this fearful time, a number of men with their families and a few slaves, took advantage of a momentary lull in the terrors of the period, to save themselves. They purchased a number of vessels, and loading each with tools, seeds, animals, valued manuscripts, and all that they possessed worth moving, started to seek a land in which they might colonize, there in time to found a new empire beyond the reach of all barbarians. They passed out of the Mediterranean and down the west coast of Africa. Fortunately they had thoroughly anticipated storms and wrecks, and each vessel was loaded in such a manner as to be independent of the others. When well on their way, one of those rare, prolonged storms from the north came on, and the vessels were soon driven far from land, and separated, each from all the others. One of these vessels managed to outlive the terrific storm, which lasted for thirty days; and when the winds abated, the hundred or more men, women, children, and slaves, found themselves among the islands of what now is named Hili-liland. There they settled - there, where nature furnishes, without labor, light and heat the year round, and vegetation is literally perpetual. They met with none of the initial difficulties of primitive peoples. They were educated, and they possessed the treasures of knowledge born of a thousand years of Roman supremacy; from the beginning they had that other priceless treasure, leisure - that real essential of perfect culture; they had for the first five hundred years no human enemy to contend with, and even then with the merest weaklings - weaklings in the hands of a people at that period very strong; for by that time the Hili-lites must have numbered a million souls, or almost as many as they now are. But of all that they possessed, the rest would have been comparatively little had they not retained in lasting memory

Charles Romyn Dake

the lesson of Rome's downfall - the price a people is compelled to pay for prolonged and unbroken luxurious indolence. This lesson of the downfall of Rome they never forgot; and to-day, with all their beauty and refinement, physical and mental effeminacy is left solely to the women. True, it requires from each inhabitant but a few hours of labor in the year to supply all purely physical material wants; but, beginning with the year of the settlement of Hili-li, up to the present time, the wealthiest in the land has performed his share of physical labor quite as conscientiously as has the poorest. Then with them, a man or woman is educated up to the time of death. The children are taught as with us, and the young men, and the young women, too, take a college course. But after the college course, they go on with their study. A great jurist at forty, or for that matter at seventy, concludes to make an exhaustive study of astronomy - or, if earlier in life he has exhausted all desire to know the facts of astronomy, he perhaps begins a study of anatomy - or whatever it may happen to please his fancy to investigate. The Hili-lites claim that in this way those who live to seventy or eighty acquire a fairly good general education, but of this I have my doubts. After the age of twenty, a man does not devote more than two hours a day to new branches of learning; but two hours a day is sufficient time, if well employed, to keep his mind always young and vigorous; and it has been shown by this people that a person under such a system retains more of the buoyancy and freshness of youth at eighty than do we in Europe and America at the age of fifty.

"In Hili-liland the people have gone much farther than we in the development of the purely reasoning faculties - in fact, they have gone so far that they now ignore reason almost completely, having carried its development to a finality, and found it comparatively worthless in the practical affairs of life. They claim - and seem by their lives to prove - that, practically, society is happier and more moral when it exists without any pretence that it is controlled by anything else than by feeling - that is, as a matter of course, by properly educated feeling. Hili-li is a kingdom, but its people must, from what I can learn, have as pure and perfect a constitutional liberty as it is possible for mankind to enjoy - not liberty as the accident of a royal whim, but such a perfect liberty as the people of England are approaching, and in which by another century they will be able to indulge themselves. They claim that as liberty does not mean license, so government of self by feeling and not by reason need not mean license - and never will mean license when correctly understood and properly directed - and yet that such government alone brings complete happiness. This putting aside and dwarfing of the reasoning faculty seems to have resulted in an intuitional state of mind. Peters says that the Hili-lites always seemed to know what he was thinking about, and were always able to anticipate and thwart his acts when they so desired.

"As I was able to gain from Peters in so brief a time a very limited range of fact from which to make correct deductions of importance, I did not expend much of that valuable time in seeking for descriptions of buildings; but I did learn sufficient in that direction to satisfy me that, to the fund of architectural knowledge brought by the ancestors of this people from Europe, they had, during the centuries, added much that is new and valuable, even sublime and truly marvellous.

"But even here in this paradise on earth, there is a criminal class - not very terrible, but, legally, a criminal class. It seems that a portion of the old, restless, warrior-spirit must have trickled along in obscure by-ways of the sanguineous system of many of these people, for among the youths of each generation several thousand out of the whole population (residing on a hundred islands, large and small), would, despite every effort of their elders, become unmanageable. These - after each young man had been given two or three opportunities to reform, and in the end been judged incorrigible - were banished to the mountain-ranges which surround the great active surface-crater already described, and which are from thirty to eighty miles distant from the Capital of Hili-li. There they might either freeze or roast, as taste should dictate.

"To-morrow evening," concluded Bainbridge, "I shall relate some particulars in the lives of Pym and Peters in Hili-liland. The purely personal experiences of these two adventurers I should ignore, were it not that they take us into the region of the wonderful crater and its peculiar surrounding mountains and valleys, where we shall see nature in one of the strangest of her many strange guises." Then, after a second's pause:

"Do you accompany me to see the poor old fellow, tomorrow?"

I promised that I would; and we agreed upon two o'clock as the time for starting. Five minutes later Doctor Bainbridge arose, and saying good-night, left me until the morrow.

THE TWELFTH CHAPTER

The next evening at the appointed hour Doctor Bainbridge came in. I had not been able to accompany him in his daily visit to Peters. As Bainbridge took his seat he said a few words concerning the old sailor, who, to the surprise, I think, of both physicians, appeared to be recovering. They hoped for scarcely more than a temporary improvement, but a little longer life for the poor old man seemed now assured.

Doctor Bainbridge glanced at the map of Hili-li, which I had spread out on the table, and began:

"In the ducal palace," said he, "in which through the kindness of the younger members of the household, Pym and Peters were permitted to reside - at first only in the servants' quarters - the servants, however, being, at least in social manners, equal to the strangers - there were, besides the immediate family of the duke, many more or less close family connections. Among these was a young woman, corresponding in her period of life to New England women in their twentieth or twenty-first year, but really in her sixteenth year. Now I should imagine from the actions of that old sea-dog, Peters, lying there in his seventy-eighth or seventy-ninth year, and forty-nine years after he last set eyes on the young woman, that she must have been the loveliest being in a land of exceeding loveliness. Her eyes, the old man says, were in general like a tropical sky in a dead calm, but on occasions they resembled a tropical sky in a thunder-storm. She had one of those broad faces in which the cheeks stand out roundly, supporting in merriment a hundred

Charles Romyn Dake

changing forms, and laughing dimples enough to steal a heart of adamant - the loveliest face, when it is lovely, in all the world. Her hair was golden, but of the very lightest of pure gold - a golden white; and when in the extreme warmth of her island home she sat amid the trees, and it was allowed to fall away in rippling waves - to what then am I to liken it? It was transcendently beautiful. I think that I can feel its appearance. It must have looked like the sun's shimmer on the sea-foam from which rose Aphrodite; or like the glint from Cupid's golden arrow-heads as, later, sitting by the side of Aphrodite, he floated along the shores of queenly Hellas, in gleeful mischief shooting landward and piercing many a heart. Ah, love in youth! The cold reasoning world shall never take away that charm; and when the years shall cover with senile snows those who have felt it, then Intuition and not Reason shall give Faith to them as the only substitute for glories that have faded and gone.

"But the form of this lovely being - what shall I say of her form! Here I pause. When Peters, at my urgent solicitation, attempted to describe it, he simply gurgled away into one of his spells of delirium. It was no use to try - though I did, again and again, try to draw from the old man something definite. It seems that she was so rounded and so proportioned as to meet every artistic demand, and to divert even from her beautiful face the glance of her enraptured beholders. If we are to gain an approximate idea of a figure so perfect, we must try to conceive what might be the result of a supreme effort of nature to show by comparison to the most artistic of her people just what puling infants they were in their attempts to create forms of true beauty from marble.

"Her name was Lilama.

"It appears that young Pym was at this time a handsome fellow, almost six feet tall; and in his attire, of which I have spoken as resembling in many respects that of the court *habitues* of Louis XIV, he was indeed a fine example of natural and artificial beauty combined. And then, he had suffered!

Need I say more? What heart of maiden would not have softened to this stranger youth?

"Well, these two loved. From what Peters tells me, the episode of Romeo and Juliet sinks into insignificance by the side of the story of their love. With leisure and with opportunity to love, for several months these young people enjoyed an earthly heaven which it is rarely indeed the lot of a young couple to enjoy. But alas! and alas! True as in the days when moonlight fell amid the palaces of Babylon and Nineveh is the old poetic expression - its truth older than Shakespeare, older than historic man - that 'The course of true love never did run smooth.'

"It seems that among the so-called criminal exiles to the Volcanic Mountains was a young man of good family, who had known - and of course loved - Lilama. And I will say in passing that the youths who comprised this class would, the larger part of them, never have been exiles, if Hili-li had required a standing army, or had even not forbidden by law the more rough and dangerous games to be played - I allude to some very rough sports and pastimes, in which bones were frequently broken - games which these youths and preceding generations of youths had initiated and developed. But there was in Hili-li, aside from boating, no allowable means for the gratification of that desire to contend with danger which is inherent in manly youths the world over. Hence these young men were by their very nature compelled to violate laws thus unnatural, and, as generally happens, in doing so they went to extremes. The young Hili-lite to whom I have alluded had been for more than a year with the exiles. His name was Ahpilus. Lilama did not reciprocate his love. She had known him from infancy, and for her there was no romance in poor Ahpilus. But the young Hili-lite was madly infatuated with her, and it seems by later developments that his enforced absence from her had driven him almost, if not wholly, insane.

"Thus stood matters about three months after the arrival in Hili-li of the Americans. It will be remembered that, according

Charles Romyn Dake

to Poe's account, Pym and Peters passed through the 'great white curtain' on March 22d. Peters says that this statement is probably correct. That date corresponds to their autumnal equinox - about. Three months later corresponds to our summer solstice - their midwinter. By the latter time, and for weeks before, the antarctic sun never rose above the horizon. But this season was in Hili-li the most beautiful and enjoyable period of the year. The open crater of almost pure white boiling lava which I have described, and which presented a surface of the most brilliant light, covering an area of more than 150 square miles, was amply sufficient to light islands from 45 to 75 miles distant. Hili-li received some direct light from a hundred or more volcanic fires - two within its own shores; but by far the greater illumination came from the reflected light of the great central lake of boiling lava. The sky, constantly filled with a circle of high-floating clouds formed of volcanic dust, the circumference of which blended away beyond the horizon, but in the centre of which, covering a space the diameter of which was about thirty miles, was a circle of light of about the same brilliancy as that of the moon, but in appearance thousands of times larger. From this overhanging cloud (the City of Hili-li lay under a part of its circumference) came during the antarctic winter a mild and beautiful light, whiter than moonlight, and lighting the island to many times the brilliancy of the brightest moonlight, though quite subdued in comparison with that which would have been derived from the sun if directly in the zenith. Peters says that the illumination in Hili-li at its midwinter was about as intense as with us on a densely cloudy day; the light not, however, being grayish, but of a pure white, now and again briefly tinted with orange, green, red, blue, and shades of other colors, caused by local and temporary outbursts of those colors in the enormous crater fires.

"I will digress for a moment longer from the relation of those occurrences which developed out of Pym's love affair, to say a word concerning some of the physical effects of this artificial light, and to explain certain facts related by Poe in his narrative of the earlier adventures of our younger hero - I say of our younger hero, because I cannot determine in my own mind which of the two, Pym or Peters, deserves to be called the hero of their strange adventures.

"On the island of Hili-li the mean summer temperature was about 12 deg. Or 13 deg. Fahrenheit higher than that of winter. The almost steady temperature of the island in winter was 93 deg. F. - occasionally dropping two or three degrees, and, very rarely, rising one or two degrees. The extremes in temperature during the year were caused by the sun's relative position - constant sunlight in summer, and its complete absence in winter. Each year, by December - the south-polar midsummer month - vegetation has become colored; and its delicacy yet brilliancy of tintage is then very beautiful, and varied beyond that of perhaps any other spot in the world. Peters has travelled over much of the tropics and subtropics, and he says that only in Florida has he seen anything to compare with the beauty of Hili-li vegetation in October and November. I should imagine from what he says that the coloring of vegetation is in great part the merest tintage, the large admixture of white giving to it a startling luminosity, and permitting the fullest effect of those neutral tints which are capable of combinations at once so restful and so pleasing to the refined eye. In the vegetation of Florida there is luminosity; but chromatic depth, as in most tropical coloring, is the chief characteristic of its visual effect. To hear Peters talk of the flowers of Hili-li, almost half a century after he himself viewed them, is a sympathetic treat to my sense of color. But for strangeness - and it was not without its element of beauty, too - the vegetable growth of July and August in that peculiar land must exceed anything else of the kind known to man. Think for a moment of the effect on vegetable growth of warmth and moisture, a rich soil, and the complete absence of sunlight! From the middle of their winter to its close, though vegetation is luxuriant, it is colorless; that is to say, it is apparently of a pure white, though, on comparison, the faintest shades of hue are discernible - a very light gray and a cream color prevailing. The peculiar grass of Hili-li, probably not indigenous yet certainly different in form from any other grass, is very tender and very luxuriant, but, even in their summer months, has a pale, almost hueless though luminous green; whilst in winter it is almost white. Many flowers bloom in the winter, but they differ one from another only in form and in odor - they are all quite hueless. And this effect of artificial heat in connection with absence of sunlight has a similar effect on animal life, the plumage of the birds being a pure white. But in the appearance of animals the summer sun does not produce much change - in that of birds, none whatever.

"This brings me to the point in Peters' story at which I may most naturally explain certain of Poe's statements - or, rather, of A. Gordon Pym's statements - which have caused more comment than any other part of the narrative. Hand me your Poe, please. - Here now: Poe says, quoting from Pym's diary:

"'On the seventeenth [of February, 1828], we set out with the determination of examining more thoroughly the chasm of black granite into which we had made our way in the first search' (this, you will recall, was on the last island upon which they set foot before being driven by winds and ocean currents farther south. They were then in hiding from the barbarians of that island, and were only a few hundred miles from the South Pole). 'We remembered that one of the fissures in the sides of this pit had been partially looked into, and we were anxious to explore it, although with no expectation of discovering here any opening. We found no great difficulty in reaching the bottom of the hollow as before, and were now sufficiently calm to survey it with some attention. It was, indeed, one of the most singular-looking places imaginable, and we could scarcely bring ourselves to believe it altogether the work of nature.' He proceeds to explain that the sides of the abyss had apparently never been connected, one surface being of soapstone, the other of black marl. The average breadth between the two cliffs was sixty feet. Here are Pym's own words again: 'Upon arriving within fifty feet of the bottom [of the abyss], a perfect regularity commenced. The sides were now entirely uniform in substance, in color and in lateral direction, the material being a very black and shining granite, and the distance between the two sides, at all points, facing each other, exactly twenty yards.' The diary goes on to state that they explored three chasms, and that in a fissure of the third of these Peters discovered some 'singular-looking indentures in the surface of the black marl forming the termination of the cul-de-sac.' It is surmised by Pym and Peters that the first of these indentures is possibly the intentional representation of a human figure standing erect, with outstretched arm; and that the rest of them bore a resemblance to alphabetical characters - such, at least, it seems from Pym's diary, was the 'idle opinion' of Peters.

[Footnote: See Narrative of A. Gordon Pym, in any complete edition of Poe's Works.]

"Pym later had a clew to the meaning of these characters, and no doubt recorded the facts in a later diary, many of the pages of which Poe never saw. But if Pym and Peters had analyzed more closely the indentures, they might have gained at least the shadow of an idea of the meaning of these representations. Pym made a copy of them, as you know, and Poe here gives us a fac-simile of that copy in his Narrative. Peters now knows in a general way of what these indentures were significant, and I will in a moment explain to you their general meaning; but first look at this fac-simile."

I drew up my chair to the side of Doctor Bainbridge, and together we looked at the representation of these indentures which Poe has furnished us. Bainbridge continued:

"Now look at this first figure, which Pym says 'might have been taken for the intentional, though rude, representation of a human figure standing erect, with outstretched arm.' The arm, observe, is here - the arm and forearm, to my mind, separated; and directly above and parallel with the arm is an arrow; and if we trace out the points of the compass as described in the diary, we find that the arm is pointing to the south, the arrow is pointing to the north; or in other words, the arm points to Hili-li; the arrow, by inference, back to the island on which the indentures exist. Now among most savages the arrow, as a symbol, represents war - a fight - individual or even tribal death.

"Many centuries preceding the time at which Pym and Peters stood examining the indentures in the black marl, and at least five centuries after the foundation of Hili-li, the natives of that zone of islands almost surrounding the South Pole at a distance of from three hundred to seven hundred miles, were affected by one of those waves of feeling which perhaps once in a thousand or several thousand years sweeps aside all the common inclinations of a people, and for some reason which lies buried in unfathomable mystery moves them to a concerted action not only unknown in the past of those who participate in it, but, so far as can be conceived, also unknown to the ancestors of the actors. Such a wave of impulse, when it comes, seems to affect all the individuals of every division of a race. In the example to which I am alluding, the impulse seemed spontaneously to move the inhabitants of islands far apart, and apparently not in communication - certainly not in direct communication. With the singleness of purpose and uniformity of action seen in an army under command of a leader, the natives of a hundred antarctic islands swarmed into ten thousand fragile boats, and directed their course toward the south. Why toward the south? Did instinct tell them that by such a course the various bands would converge to a union? They knew not. The first few boats arrived at Hili-li. Nine of every ten of those that began the journey were lost - but still, boats continued to arrive at the islands of the Hili-li group. Then, and after five hundred years of peace, the Hili-lites saw that they were to be overrun by barbarians, as their history told them their ancestors had once, in distant lands, been overrun. The Hili-lites did not have formidable weapons; but fortunately those of the invaders were scarcely more efficient. The conflict came to a hand to hand engagement. The invaders could not return, even had they so desired; so they must fight and win, or die. The Hili-lites had no place of retreat, even had they been willing to flee; and they too must fight and win, or die. The invaders numbered more than a hundred thousand men; the Hili-lites, about forty thousand that were able to fight in such a battle. The latter armed themselves with clubs about four feet long, one inch in diameter at the handle, two inches in diameter at the farther extremity, and made of a wood similar to the dense tropical lignum-vitae (almost an inconceivable growth in that comparatively sunless region); and, for additional weapons, behind natural and artificial barriers they heaped piles of lava-blocks, sharp, jagged, and weighing each from one to five pounds. The invaders had a few very flimsy bows, scarcely six arrows to each bow - and nothing else in the way of weapons. From all sides, on came the invaders in their frail boats, in one mad rush upon the main island of Hili-li, where the Hili-lites had, including their women, children, and aged men, gathered.

"The invaders were ill-fed, tired out by a sea-voyage exhausting almost past comprehension, ignorant, almost weaponless, and making a charge in small boats; whilst for them the favorable elements in the coming battle were that they possessed five men for each two of the defenders, and were impelled by a mad, instinctive impulse to advance, similar to that of a swarm of migratory locusts, which advances even through fire, and though it require the charred bodies of ninety-nine thousand of their number over which the remaining thousand may cross. The Hili-lites were well-fed, not fatigued, intelligent, comparatively well-armed, and were on land, prepared for the battle; whilst they possessed also the inherited Roman spirit, once lost by their ancestors, but by the descendants recovered amid new and pure surroundings.

"Before a landing could be made, half the invaders, in the confusion incident to a bombardment with lava-blocks, were thrown from their boats and drowned, or knocked on the head as they swam ashore. Of the other half, a third were killed as they attempted to land, and another third within five minutes after they reached the shore. Then the remaining fifteen thousand or more rushed back to their boats, only to find them sunk in the shallow water near the shore - it having been quite easy for eight or ten Hili-lites to sink each boat, by bearing in unison their weight on one gunwale - a thousand or two young Hili-lites having been assigned to that duty. Then the poor wretches who remained threw down their flimsy bows, and fell face-downward on the ground, at the feet of the victors. Under the circumstances, what could so noble a people as were the Hili-lites do? They could not slaughter in cold blood nearly twenty thousand trembling human creatures. So it was finally decided to build a thousand large-sized row-boats, and it being the best time of the year for that purpose, take them back to their own islands. This was done. But in punishment for their offence, and as a constant reminder of the existence of the Hili-lites - (who, as these savages knew, had destroyed more than eighty thousand of their number, with a loss of only twelve of their own killed, and thirty-seven seriously wounded - which fact, by the bye, Peters says is inscribed on a monument in the City of Hili-li, as well as recorded in the official history of the Hili-lites) - as a constant reminder, I say, of a people so powerful, they were ordered never, on any island in their group, to display any object of a white color - the national color of the Hili-lites. So strict and inclusive was this command, that the natives were ordered to take each of their descendants as soon as his teeth appeared, and color them with an indelible, metallic blue-black dye, repeating the operation every year up to ten, and thereafter once in five years. The command closed with the statement that the natives would be allowed to retain the whites of their eyes, but only for the reason that, as they looked at each other they would there, and only there, see the national color of Hili-li, and so have always in mind the promise of the victors, that if another descent on Hili-li were ever attempted, no single native - man, woman, or child - would be allowed to live. In addition to this, the Hili-lites engraved on a number of suitable rocks on each island an inscription, briefly recording a reminder of the terrible results of this attempt at conquest, heading each inscription with the rude representation of a man with arm extended to the south, over which and parallel with which was placed an arrow pointing to the north - meaning, 'There is the direction in which a certain foolish people may go to find quick death: from there comes war and extermination!'

"So effective were the means employed by the Hili-lites to prevent future raids, that, though the inhabitants of these islands had again increased, probably to a million or more, no second invasion had ever been attempted by even the strongest and bravest of their savage chiefs."

"Well," I said, as Bainbridge paused, and seemed to be thinking just what to say next, "what of the beautiful Lilama and the infatuated Ahpilus? I hope poor Pym is not to have so charming a love-feast broken into by any untoward event. I must say, Bainbridge, those Hili-lites were wonderfully careless of their loveliest women - of a beautiful girl of sixteen, and so close to royalty itself."

"Well, my cold-blooded friend, what will you say when I tell you that Lilama was an orphan, and had inherited from her father the only island in the archipelago upon which precious stones were found, and that even in that strange land she was wealthier than the king? Had she been able to get the products of her islands into the markets of the world, she would have been wealthier than Croesus, the Count of Monte Cristo and the Rothschilds, all combined. However, in Hili-li, wealth was not - well, not an all-powerful factor; important, but not having the power which in the remainder of the civilized world it possesses. To have power, money must be able to purchase human labor or its products, as only by human power is all other force utilized. In Hili-li, a citizen possessed everything that he required for his ordinary wants, and it was almost impossible to purchase the leisure time of any man. It was possible on certain conditions to procure human labor, but it was extremely difficult to do so. Then, for seven or eight hundred years slavery had been prohibited in the land, all existing slaves having been emancipated - after which, in the course of a few generations, Hili-lian history says, the slaves and the slave-spirit were lost in the mass of the population.

"In thinking over the position of Lilama and Pym, you must consider that the older members of the family would probably not soon hear of such a thing as love between these two, and,

Charles Romyn Dake

even when they did hear of it, would have little doubt of being able to 'control the situation' as they should please. Then, with the ideas possessed by the Hili-lites, there would not arise any very serious objection to a union by marriage of Lilama and young Pym. The Hili-lites believed the feelings to be a guide to true happiness; and whilst they would certainly have controlled the circumstances leading up to the seemingly unwise marriage of a girl of sixteen - for they believed also in a proper education of the feelings - they would not have prevented even a seemingly unwise marriage, provided the feelings of those concerned loudly demanded such a union - I mean that if in *reason* such a marriage should seem unwise - But enough. The hour is late, and I shall not before to-morrow evening at eight o'clock begin a description of the exciting scenes through which the beautiful Lilama was so soon to pass, and the adventures of Pym and Peters - adventures so terrible that for centuries to come they will descend, a thrilling romance, from generation to generation, in those usually quiet and peaceful islands."

And then, against my protest, he took his departure.

THE THIRTEENTH CHAPTER

The following morning, after leaving the hotel on some trifling errand, I returned to find Arthur awaiting me. He stood by my table, and occupied himself in turning the leaves of one of my books. He was looking with much interest at a picture in a work on paleontology, a book which by some chance had accompanied a few selected works that I had brought with me from England. The picture that so interested him, I saw as I drew nearer, represented the skeleton of a prehistoric mammoth with a man standing by its side, the latter figure placed in the picture, no doubt, for the purpose of showing relations of size. As I stepped up close to Arthur's side, he turned a page in the book and disclosed a still more startling representation, that of a reconstructed mammoth, wool, long coarse hair, enormous tusks, and the rest. Arthur, with his usual curiosity, wanted to be told "all about it," and I with my usual desire to teach the searcher after knowledge even of little things - though a mammoth is scarcely a "little thing" - briefly gave him some insight of the subject, running over the differences between the mastodontine and the elephantine mammoth; and then remarked to him, incidentally, that an American *mastodon giganteus*, found not far from where we stood, over in Missouri, a third of a century before, was now in our British Museum, where I had seen it. Of course Arthur had many questions to ask concerning the "gigantic-cus" which I had actually seen. I gave him, from memory, the best description possible, telling him that it was more than twenty feet in length, about ten feet high, and so on. He seemed very thoughtful for several moments, whilst I sat down to look at

Charles Romyn Dake

my morning paper. After somewhat of a pause, he asked permission to speak - for with all Arthur's lack of cultivation he was not wanting in a sense of propriety, which he usually displayed in his relations with those whom he liked. I gave the desired permission, when he said,

"I just wanted to say, sir, that I wish't you'd let me come up of an evenin' and sit off in the corner there on that chair, and hear Doctor Bainbridge tell about Pym and Peters. I know you've been mighty good to tell me the most of it so far, but to-night he'll tell how that beautiful female loves Pym, like you said early this morning he was goin' to; and I'm awful anxious to hear soon. Something big's goin' to happen, and I pity the natives if they rouse up that orang-outang Peters. You said I would disturb the flowin' of Doctor Bainbridge's retorick by goin' out and in. But I won't go out. I just won't go out; if the Boss don't like it he can lump it - I can quit. Right down the street I can rent a little shop-room, and a feller and me has been talking of startin' a ice-cream saloon for the summer - yes, I can quit if the Boss don't like it. I work all day, and half the night; I can't keep up my system with a single drink without there's a kick a-coming; and now if I can't have a little literature when it's right in the house, it's a pity. No: I'll not interrup' the retorick."

Well, the end of it was, I gave my consent; and Arthur went off delighted. I mention these facts in explanation of my position. It has been said by one who ought to know, and the statement has been often enough quoted to evidence some general belief in its truth, that consistency is a jewel. I had said, that, during Doctor Bainbridge's recitations of Dirk Peters' story, Arthur should not be present; and now that he will be seen in a corner of my room evening after evening, I desire that the reader shall know all the circumstances.

That afternoon I accompanied Bainbridge on his visit to the aged sailor. I was pleased to see the old *lusus naturae* sitting in a chair, and seemingly quite strong. Bainbridge made himself agreeable, delivered to Peters some small gifts of edibles, and then proceeded to ask a number of questions - I presume, from their nature, concerning *minutiae* relating to the adventures under consideration. Then we returned to town, and separated.

Promptly at eight o'clock Bainbridge entered, and, as he took his customary seat, cast a glance at Arthur, who sat on a chair in the corner of the room.

"Well," began Bainbridge, after a moment's thought, "we were remarking that within our own knowledge and experience, true love has been exceedingly likely to meet with obstructions to its complete fruition: - and Lilama and Pym met with a similar experience in far-away Hili-li. Peters took a great interest in Pym's love affair; in fact, he had grown almost to worship the young fellow whose life he had many times preserved, and who in less than a year had, under his eye, grown from a careless boy to a thoughtful man. Pym returned the liking of his old companion and benefactor; but Peters' sentiment was one of infatuation, such as only those persons who are 'close to nature' seem capable of feeling in its fullest development. When the feeling of which I speak exists in its most intense form, it includes a devotion equal to that of the dog for its master: it is wholly instinctive, and not even the certainty that death stalks in the path between can keep it from its object.

"One morning early, there was excitement in the ducal palace. Lilama was missing. Search was diligently made. Pym was wild with excitement; and as the morning wore on Peters grew almost mad. (I shall speak of morning, afternoon, evening, and night. The degree of light in Hili-li did not now vary in the twenty-four hours; but it is necessary that I should in some manner divide the day, and our usual method seems the best.) The Duke himself arrived at about ten o'clock, by which time the search had ceased, and what to do next had become the question. The Duke appeared surprised at something, and spoke a few words to his son, a young man of twenty-two or twenty-three, by name Diregus, who thereupon looked slightly foolish, as one does who has made some puerile mistake. The Duke appeared to feel a real touch of pity for Pym, who sat dejected, a picture of intense anguish, now and then casting a beseeching look at the Duke - the only person who, to his mind, might be able to assist him to regain his sweetheart. The Duke again spoke to his son, who, turning to Pym, motioned him to accompany them. Then, followed by Peters, they walked down to the shore, and entered a boat.

"From the moment of starting, every movement of the Hili-lites seemed as if prearranged. It was a peculiarity of this people that a number of them acting together talked very little, each of the party appearing to know the wishes and intentions of the others, without a word spoken. And so was it on this occasion. Scarcely a word was uttered, and each seemed to comprehend the wishes of the others, mainly by glances and by semi-involuntary movements. In the present instance, father and son did not once glance at each other, yet the son was evidently aware of each wish of the father. They finally came to a landing, across the bay, in the suburbs of the city most distant from the locality in which stood the ducal palace. There, some four hundred feet from the shore, amid giant trees, in spacious and seemingly neglected grounds, stood a very large residence, evidently many centuries old, and of a style of architecture not seen by the Americans elsewhere in Hili-li. The building had an eerie look, and as the party drew near to it Peters observed that but one of its wings was inhabited, the remainder of the mansion being in a state of almost complete decay. They all entered by a side doorway into the inhabited wing. Pym and Peters were motioned to seats in the hallway, the Duke remarking, in hushed tones, 'The home of Masusaelili,' as he and Diregus passed through a broken and decaying doorway into apartments beyond. Soon Diregus returned, and, escorting Pym and Peters through several disordered rooms, finally paused before a large curtained doorway. Then Diregus spoke, but in a hushed voice, and with an awed solemnity that chilled his hearers through and through.

"'Fear not,' he said; 'no harm will befall you. If the benign Fate is to smile - well; if the Furies are to rage, we can but bow to the Will that has held in its hand for countless cycles this petty planet - a grain in the wastes of Eternity. Come!'

"He passed through the doorway, and the two followed him. The room they entered was spacious - almost thirty feet square. It was crowded with strange devices, and was lighted by six colored swinging globes. A strange odor filled the atmosphere of the apartment. The room was brilliantly enough illuminated, though the light was variously colored and its shades and blendings were confusing; whilst the strange, intoxicating perfume also helped to perplex the senses. If the apartment had contained not more than several objects, the visitors might soon have detected and observed all of them; but, as it was, Pym and Peters stood gazing confusedly about them, momentarily beholding fresh objects, all of them strange, many of them bizarre, some of them frightful. It was apparently at the same instant of time that the sight of Pym and Peters fell upon an object so awesome that their hearts almost ceased to beat, and then bounded on with throbs that sent the cold blood leaping down their spines and to their scalps in chilling waves that ceased only when their terror reached the numbing stage. There before them, not six feet away, among great cubes of crystal, and vast retorts, and enormous vase-like objects on the floor, stood an aged man. How aged? He was old when the antarctic barbarians were slain, and their remnant sent back to its home on those dreary islands to live forever in blackness. None knew how old he was - they, the rulers, knew not; or if they did, on that subject they were silent. Some said that on the ship which brought the nucleus of their race from Rome, came Masusaelili with the others - an aged man, the oldest on the vessel. There he stood before the visitors, his white beard trailing on the tiling at his feet, his shrunken form erect. But, whence the terror? Three times ere I could learn this fact (and even then I learned it more by inference than by words) did Peters sink into delirium, muttering, 'Oh, those eyes - the eyes of a god - of a god of gods.' The aged man seated himself at a small Roman table, and, turning to the Duke without a question, said in a voice unlike any other voice in all the world - steady, but thin, high-pitched, sharp, penetrating and agitating depths within the hearer never reached before,

"'You come for knowledge of The Lily. Behold!'

"He pointed to a cube of crystal near him, which, Peters will swear, was a moment earlier perfectly transparent. But now it looked as if filled with milk of purest whiteness. As they gazed at it, a fire appeared in the centre; and soon around the fire there sprang into being a circular range of mountains, and on the side of one of these - the nearest - stood two persons.

"'Lilama - Ahpilus,' screamed Diregus; 'he has stolen her away!'

"Yes: for though Pym and Peters had never seen the exiled lover, they recognized Lilama; and even they could surmise the rest.

"'The youth is mad,' said the Duke. 'We must rescue our darling from the maniac.'

"Pym, in his impatience, was about to rush from the room; but the old man beckoned for him to approach. He did as desired. Then the aged man placed a hand upon Pym's head, and drew it down to him; and the man who had lived thousands of years whispered some words into the ear of the youth who had lived not yet four lustrums. As Peters described for me in his homely way the change that came over the face of Pym as that human millenarian spoke perhaps one hundred words into the young man's ear, I was reminded of reading as a boy, some years ago, a description of the burning somewhere in South America of a great cathedral. The fire occurred during a morning service, and with the alarm the doorways of the building were at once obstructed by a mass of struggling humanity. Some two or three thousand persons were consumed in this terrible holocaust. The correspondent who wrote the description of the fire of which I speak said that for ten minutes he stood outside the cathedral after the surrounding heat had become so intense that efforts at rescue ceased, and from a raised spot he looked through the windows from which the glass had crumbled - looked across the great window-sills raised eight feet from the cathedral floor, looked into the faces of the doomed. And as he gazed, he saw the faces of many maidens with their lovers by their side - (it was a gala day, and all were in their best attire). As he looked, within a brief ten minutes he saw horror-stricken eyes gaze at the approaching fire, and at other victims sixty feet away already burning; then quickly would the fire approach the owner of those eyes, reach him, consume him: And in those fleeting moments the face of a young girl would pass through every stage from youth to extreme age, and then sink down in death. As the aged mystic whispered to Pym, the young man's face turned ghastly, then worked convulsively, then settled into firm resolve. And Peters never again saw on the face of the youth whom he loved with the love of a mother and of a father in one - never again saw the old, careless, boyish smile. Did the old man - shall we call him a man? - did the old man whisper into Pym's ear the secret of eternity? Would such a revelation have changed youth to manhood in a hundred seconds?

"As Pym was led by Diregus from the room, Peters started to follow; but the aged mystic motioned for him, too, to approach. Peters says that after what he had just seen he felt much more like taking to flight than he did like obeying the summons; but he obeyed it. The old man pointed to one of the smaller crystal cubes, which would have measured some five feet across. As Peters gazed upon it, it began to take on the milky hue which he had before witnessed. Peters says that at first he thought these cubes were of solid crystal, but after he witnessed the strange alterations of which they were capable, he believed they were hollow. He continued to gaze as directed, and soon he saw, sitting at a table, with a lighted candle by her side, knitting, his poor old mother, from whose side he had, fifteen years before, when a thoughtless, wicked boy, ran away to sea. He had never seen her again - he has not

Charles Romyn Dake

seen her again to the present day. As he gazed upon that aged, wrinkled face - that hard, Indian face (his mother was a civilized Indian), he saw that look which man sees nowhere else on sea or land save only in a mother's face. He threw himself face-downward on the floor, and wrung in agony his hands, and moaned out pleas for forgiveness; but the poor, old, fragile form knitted on, and on, and the face was never raised. Alas! why must we all feel the full force of a mother's love and sacrifices only when too late? Why must it be that the deepest of all unselfish love goes ever unrewarded?

"Peters scarcely knows how he got from the room. He staggered out into the grounds, and saw that the remainder of the party were already seated in the boat.

"But I must hasten on. Let me say in a few words, that the party returned to the ducal palace, and immediately prepared to rescue Lilama from the power of her discarded lover, the exiled Ahpilus. The rescue party, on the advice of the Duke, was small. He explained to Peters that so far as mere human force was concerned, a thousand men could never rescue the maiden. Her return to them, alive and in health, would depend upon strategy, or possibly might be accomplished as a result of some superhuman individual effort. He was of opinion, he remarked - and he judged from what he had been told by government officials lately returned from 'Crater Mountains' and also from changes in the young man observed by himself preceding the sentence of banishment - that Ahpilus was a maniac. The Duke went on to say that he really felt but little hope of ever again seeing, alive, his loved young 'cousin.' Then he explained that, whilst there were spots on 'Crater Mountains,' from five to eight miles from the central crater, on the far side of the nearer hills, hot enough to roast a large animal, there were other spots on the far side of the remoter mountain ranges where, protected from crater radiation and exposed to antarctic air-currents, the temperature was almost always far below the freezing-point, and sometimes so cold that no animal life, even antarctic animal life, could endure it for an hour. He said that poor Lilama was lost, unless some other exile should save her - which was unlikely, even if possible - or unless we could invent some plan of capture so peculiar as to baffle the madman - a man, by the bye, of enormous physical strength, and with a madman's cunning. Peters stood drinking in every word spoken by the Duke; whilst Pym listened as if heartbroken, but in an impatient, anxious way, indicative of a restless impulse to be gone. The Duke continued to instruct and advise them, until a large sail-boat was provisioned and manned, when the rescue party hastened away on its errand of love and mercy.

"The party consisted of the young man Diregus, Lilama's cousin; of Pym and Peters; and of six boatmen, who might or might not be employed directly in the attack and rescue, as should later seem best. The party had no weapons other than a few peculiarly-shaped clubs, similar to those mentioned by me in describing the fight of the early Hili-lites against the invading barbarians, and a long dirk-knife in the possession of Peters.

"By glancing at this map of Hili-liland, you will observe that the sea-course to 'Crater Mountains' was almost direct, it lying in a straight line out of Hili-li Bay and across the open sea for thirty miles. They were to enter 'Volcano Bay,' which pursued a tortuous course amid the mountains, until they should reach a certain pass between two of the highest mountains in the whole range. In the centre of one of these mountains was a peak some eight miles high, named by the founders of Hili-li 'Mount Olympus.' It was possible to sail (or to push their boat) to within seven miles of a point where the lavabed was still red hot - about thirteen miles from the edge of the central, white-hot, boiling lava. This, however, they did not do; first, because the pass mentioned, which was the best course up into the mountains, began about three or four miles short of the inner extremity of Volcano Bay; and second, because within a mile or two of that extremity the water of the bay sometimes actually boiled, and the heat would there be quite unendurable."

Charles Romyn Dake

Here Bainbridge paused for a moment, and then continued, "Well, my attentive friend, 'the witching hour' approaches. We lost too much time in discussion this evening - What! only ten o'clock?" he said, looking at his watch. "Well, I am at a good resting-place in the story, anyway, as you will to-morrow evening admit. Why, if I started you up into those mountains to-night, we should get no sleep before daylight. No, no: 'sufficient unto the day is the evil thereof; more I would' - how does it go? Well, it means that the evils of two days should not be crowded into one day. The attempted quotation - as generally happens when I attempt quotation from the Bible - is a double failure: not a success simply in accuracy of repetition; and, at best, not appropriate. For I have more, and a great deal more. But" - rising from his chair - "I must depart. So adieu until the morrow - and good-night to you."

He had not been gone five minutes, and I was just complimenting Arthur on his silence and otherwise commendable behavior, when Doctor Castleton bounced into the room. He knew in a general way the drift of Peters' story, up to the developments of the evening before. His curiosity to hear what Doctor Bainbridge had so patiently and laboriously gleaned from Peters did not seem intense, or it was wonderfully well suppressed. Still, he liked briefly to learn from me the outlines of the story, and had not failed to meet me at some period of each day, and to hint at a desire for information. Therefore, I knew with what object he had this evening come to see me, and I ran rapidly over the facts developed the preceding evening, and then over those of that evening.

"Yes, yes," he said, "I see, I see. Rich people, but money no good; poor people, but poverty no hardship. That's Bainbridge's nonsense - he never got anything out of Peters along that line. Money, but money no value! Oh, well; Bainbridge is young and full of theories. The next thing he'll be saying that they've found a way in Hili-li to make life as valuable and agreeable for the lazy and the vile as for the industrious and moral classes. He's just philosophizing to suit himself. Why, a people would have money if they had to make it out of their own hides, and the money would have value, too - yes, and labor-purchasing value. No people will ever have all they want, for they will invent new wants forever, and more rapidly than the old wants can be gratified. They may get all they require of food and clothing, and that, too, in exchange for next to no work; but they will always want things that they are unable to procure. So long as people do different kinds of work - supply the community with different necessaries - they will trade; and when they trade, common-sense will soon invent a circulating medium. And so long as one man is the mental or the physical superior of another, and fills more of the demands of the community than another, he will have the means of gratifying more of his own wants than the other man; and as differences increase, and different temperaments develop their varying propensities - some anticipating their ability to expend, others desiring to accumulate for the everlasting rainy day - there will, and necessarily must, arise stable methods of preserving values. Oh, pshaw! Who wants to make all men - and all women, too - in a single mental and physical mould? - and a mighty insignificant mould at that? The world is not made better by ease and plenty, but by hardship. Ease and plenty come not but as a reward of striving. When every man is like every other man, and all are too lazy to want anything, the reign of money will be ended.

"Why not enroll the whole world, and have a great army in civil life, constantly under command, with the nature of its wants and their form of gratification fixed or regulated by - well, by a majority of these dough men? That's the only way I know for the people to get rid of a circulating medium, and live."

He paused for a moment, both in his locution, and in his walk back and forward across the floor. Then he resumed both:

"I do not know of anything quite so idiotic as is this howl directed against the possession of wealth. I myself am a poor man: if I do not earn a living each year, I go hungry or go in debt. But I would not trade off my chances of a competency and of wealth - a reasonable ambition for every man in England and America - no, not to see every rich man on earth starve - or even sent to hell. This howl is the mark of a plebeian, or at least of a wickedly childish cast of intellect. I know of nothing quite so foolish, and of nothing half so brutal. The Jew-baiting folly is a phase of the same nonsense. It is foolish, because if the possession of capital is denied to the men who can best acquire and hence best continue to employ it, then commercial civilization must take a back seat - in fact, go, and go to stay; and this means abject poverty for everybody but a handful of state and church aristocrats. It is brutal, because it is unreasoning and mistakenly vindictive. It is the howl of the mentally weak - of the mob; and the mob is always brutal.

"If we are to suppress those whose possessions evidence a past or a present performance of some service that the world demanded and paid for, we cast aside the useful of the earth: we know that their possessions were gained, not from the pauper, but from those who held material wealth; and I know, and can most solemnly swear, from personal experience, that in this world nobody gets anything for nothing.

"Oh, the first French revolution! The French revolution was all right. The fight was not against commercial wealth, but against a corrupt church, state, and social order. And nobody maintains that the commercial class is immaculate: every class should come under the regulation of good statutory law. I only claim that it would be wrong and foolish to take away in whole or in part the accumulations of the commercial class. With us the only wealthy citizens are commercial people, and those who have acquired wealth through them, for with us here, at this time, the wealthy owners of realty are commercial men who have put their surplus money into land. Oh, yes: control them; but it's not the business men of the world who need the most looking after."

And with that he shot out of the room and down the stairs; and I soon after retired to rest.

THE FOURTEENTH CHAPTER

The next evening at an early hour Arthur was seated in the least conspicuous corner of my room, a spot which he seemed to have selected as his own; and, as usual, Doctor Bainbridge entered promptly at eight o'clock. After the customary minute or two of thoughtful quiet, and a glance at the map of Hili-li, which each evening I kept spread on my table in the centre of the room, Bainbridge continued his recital:

"Last evening brought us to the moment when the rescue party, having entered Volcano Bay, were about to land at the foot of the great mountain, called Olympus - the Hili-li synonym for Mount preceding the name Olympus when the peak, some eight miles high, was referred to. Now if you will examine this map with a little care you will observe here, near the inner extremity of Volcano Bay, an apparently narrow inlet passing directly into the mountain-side. This does not represent an inlet from the bay, but an outlet from Crater Lake, a very deep lake, the surface of which is several thousand feet below its banks, the lake being on the top of the mountain, just south of Mt. Olympus, and emptying into Volcano Bay. This outlet is a small stream at the bottom of a chasm which cannot correctly be represented on my map, as it is relatively very narrow, being only from ten to one hundred feet in width. This chasm is what we here term a canyon, or *canon*, the walls of which in this instance rise perpendicularly from the water to the average height of ten thousand feet. The paths up the mountain are on the sides of this outlet - not close to the water, but winding in and out along the

Charles Romyn Dake

mountain-side above, there being a passable way on each side of the canyon from the bay to the lake, the distance from bay to lake along either path being, in its tortuous course, about thirteen miles. At Crater Lake the mountain rises to a height of about six miles, the surface of the lake being about four miles above the sea level, its banks some ten thousand feet in height. A perfectly straight line down the mountain-side would measure about eight or nine miles.

"As the canyon leaves the bay, its walls are about a hundred feet high, and are separated by about the same distance; but as the mountain is ascended, the walls rapidly rise, and soon become far above the water between, and they gradually approach each other. At certain points the walls actually overhang the stream below, and almost meet, at one spot approximating to within ten feet of each other. Three miles from the bay the walls are twenty feet apart, and for the remaining five miles they do not at any place approach closer, but on the other hand very gradually separate to about sixty feet at the extreme top. At five miles from the bay the walls are fully ten thousand feet in altitude, and are nowhere less in height from that point to the edge of Crater Lake.

"Our party started up the mountain on one side of this canyon, or giant chasm, Diregus appearing in some way to know that this was the proper course to pursue. When they were some three miles on their way, a young man was seen approaching, but on the opposite side of the chasm. He was a young fellow of prepossessing appearance, dressed in plain, coarse loathing, and having the elastic movement and grace of the better classes. Peters observed, when only the width of the chasm separated the two, that the young Hili-lite had a laughing eye, full of latent mischief, but also of intelligence.

"He was known to Diregus, and the two began a conversation. He was one of the exiles, by name Medosus. Diregus soon ascertained that the exiles had long known Ahpilus to be insane; that, three days before, his condition had become much aggravated, and that on the preceding day he had suffered from an attack of raving mania which lasted several hours. Medosus did not know of the abduction of Lilama, but he had three hours earlier seen Ahpilus a mile or two from Crater Lake.

"When the party heard this, they were anxious to proceed, but Medosus in turn had a few questions to ask, and in common courtesy Diregus was compelled to wait and reply to the poor exile's interrogatories.

"Whilst the two conversed, Medosus took from his pocket some dry, brown, crumpled leaves, and put a wad of them into his mouth, much as would an American planter who raises tobacco and chews the unprepared leaf. Now Peters was a lover of tobacco, and the sight of this action, so suggestive of his loved weed, excited him greatly, as he had not so much as seen a scrap of tobacco for months. When it developed that it was tobacco that Medosus had placed in his mouth, and that in some of the valleys between these mountains a species of wild tobacco grew, Peters was determined to have some of it, the craving of months seeming so near to gratification; and he asked Medosus to give him a little of it, to last until he could procure a fuller supply. Medosus was perfectly willing to grant this request; but on rolling up a wad and attempting to throw it across the chasm, it fell into the abyss and fluttered downward to the water nearly two miles below. He was about to make a second effort, when Peters stopped him, and then a pretty, though a really terrible thing happened - to relate which was the real purpose of this digression from my story proper.

"Peters was at the moment standing some fifteen feet from the edge of the chasm, the chasm being at this point about twenty feet in width - twenty feet in width, and even here, where it was two thousand feet less in depth than it was a mile higher up, at least eight thousand feet in descent - sheer to the raging torrent and the huge, jagged lava-bowlders below. It was all done so quickly that none of the party had time to become alarmed. Peters, whose arms when he hung them reached to within four inches of his feet, stooped just enough to bring his hands to the ground. Then, as a lame man using crutches might swing himself along, but with lightning-like swiftness, Peters took two rapid jumps toward the edge of the chasm, the second jump landing him directly on its edge. Then he shot up and out into the air over that awful abyss, and landed on the opposite side as gently as a cat lands from a six-foot leap; and it did not seem to require of him an unusual effort. He received his tobacco, and turned to make the leap back.

"When Peters mentioned to me the circumstance of this leap, it was only because he had at the time it was made been so interested in the incident of getting the tobacco, that he never forgot the occurrence; in fact, it seems to have impressed his mind and memory almost as deeply as did the old man with the 'snow-drift beard and the eyes of a god.'

"I attempted to get out of Peters just how he made the leap - whether with the legs or the arms, or both as an impelling force; but it was no use. I believe that he does not himself know - he did it by an animal instinct, and that is all there is to be said. The old fellow does not really know his age, but I should place it, at the present time, at from seventy-eight to eighty years, which, if correct, would indicate that he was twenty-eight or thirty at the time he was in Hili-li. He must have been as strong generally as three average men, and in the arms as strong as five or six such men. You remember telling me yourself how he twisted that iron poker, and broke the oak pole; and that was the act of an invalid nearly eighty years of age. Oh, he must have been a Samson at twenty-eight, and as agile as a tiger. What I could draw out of him concerning the leap, reminded me of descriptions I have read of the *Simiidae* - particularly of the Borneo orang-outang.

"But to return: The party separated from Medosus, who, when about two hundred feet away, shouted back, 'You'd better stay with us, Diregus. We do not here have to hide away when we play - or at - ' (mentioning the names of two very rough games prohibited by law on all the islands of the Hili-li Kingdom - games corresponding to our foot-ball and our wrestling). The party continued up the mountain-side, resting as they felt the need of rest. No preparation for the darkness of night was necessary; for here the crater-light was very bright - in some unshaded spots it was even painfully brilliant.

"After several hours of laborious ascent, the small party of four (Diregus had taken with them only one of the boatmen) came within plain sight of the rim of Crater Lake, half a mile ahead of them, and almost perpendicularly above, though nearly two miles away measured along the shortest route that travellers might pursue. It was not at the time known, and therefore never will be known, whether or not Lilama had caught a glimpse of her approaching friends; but at that moment a piercing scream rang through the air from above. Peters thinks that Lilama saw some of the party, because the quality of the scream was not such as to convey an impression that she was in instant danger. The signal, if signal it was, was not repeated, nor did the party wait for a repetition. They all hurried onward with renewed vigor; and, in a short time, considering the severity of the ascent, had reached a point near which they supposed the scream must have been uttered.

"The party had scattered, and were searching among the mammoth lava-bowlders, and in the small side valleys and fissures; Peters, however, as he then always instinctively did, keeping by the side of Pym. The two had separated to quite a distance from the others, when, being then quite close to the edge of the great chasm, they heard a deep though penetrating voice say the one word (of course in the Hili-li language), 'Well?'

"Looking in the direction from which the voice came, they saw on the opposite side of the chasm a young and handsome man, dressed much as was the exile, Medosus. There could not for a moment be any doubt in the minds of Pym and Peters concerning the identity of this young man; but if there had been, it would immediately have been dispelled.

"'Well, gentlemen?' the voice further said.

"Pym and Peters had stepped up close to the edge of the abyss, which here was, as it was throughout the upper third of its length, from forty-five to fifty-five feet in width (Peters thinks that at this part of its course it was fully fifty feet broad).

"'Well, gentlemen: why are you two, strangers to me, and to my people, also, I think - why are you here?'

"The speaker would have seemed very far from insane, had it not been for his large black eyes, shifting and glittering in the bright volcanic light.

"At last Pym spoke:

"'Sir,' he said, very calmly, 'we came to assist our friends of the neighboring island - friends who have been very kind to us - to search for a maiden who by some strange mischance has been lost from her people - from her people and her friends, who grieve sorely over their loss.'

"'Ah, ha,' said Ahpilus - for it was he - 'very good. And they grieve, do they? Curse them, let them grieve! And a certain lover - and curse him, too - does he grieve? He would better! Ah, ha, ha, ha' - the voice rising with each syllable, until the last was almost shrieked at Pym - 'Kind to you, were they? Well, there is one of them near by - on this side the chasm, curse you - who won't be kind to you again. Yes, and you may see her, too.' Then Ahpilus stepped off behind some thick, stunted bushes of a variety of evergreen, whence, in a moment, he returned, leading by the wrist Lilama. 'Great Jove above! Girl, do you see your lover over there? You have no love for me - you never had; but never again in time or in eternity shall I lie with burning brain, thinking of those snowy arms about the stranger's neck - aye, as once I saw them in the palace grounds. Curse you all, and may you all alike be d - d. Why should a stranger come through ten thousand perils to add to all my untold agonies.' Here for a moment his voice softened, almost to a gentle whisper. 'Ah, Lilama, once, only once, you shall, of your own free will, clasp those arms around me - if not in love, then in terror. A moment more, and over this abyss together we shall go!' With terror in his eyes, Pym glanced at Peters; and even the phlegmatic Peters was startled. 'Yes, for one moment in each other's arms; and then for me, the everlasting darkness of Tartarus, or of endless oblivion.'

"As he talked, he had dropped the wrist of Lilama, and she crouched upon the ground with her hands before her face, whilst Ahpilus continued to rave, and to pace from the chasm's edge away and back again, in maniac strides, until he had almost beaten where he paced a pathway. There was not the slightest necessity for Ahpilus to guard Lilama, for the awful chasm was more than twice the width that any sane and normal man, even an athlete, would dare attempt to leap, even to preserve his own life; and the distance to be traversed to gain a point in the chasm so narrow that an ordinary man would dare attempt to leap it, was several miles down the mountain-side; so that Lilama was at least ten miles beyond the reach of Pym, though less than eighty feet away.

"The mental strain on poor Pym was almost enough to make him a madman. There strode the maniac, to and from the edge of the abyss, rhythmically, rarely varying the distance by a yard - twenty yards off, then back again, then away. On every third or fourth approach he stepped literally to the edge of the chasm, and glanced down, ten thousand feet to where the stream below looked like the finest silver thread, lighted by the dazzling light from the giant crater, reflected into every smallest fissure. Now and again the madman would lash himself into a fury, and stop for a moment to gaze at Lilama, who never moved from her crouching position some ten feet from the canyon's brink. Even Peters, the stoic, was moved - but moved to anger rather than to grief or fear. He inwardly chafed, and madly raved, by turns, at the impotency of his position; whilst Pym seemed frozen into statuesque despair. How much longer would this scene of terror last? Oh, the thought of that awful leap into space! The maniac might any moment end the scene - each time as he approached in that wild rush backward and forward might be the last. The

Charles Romyn Dake

slightest move, the slightest sound, might precipitate the dire calamity - and Lilama as well as Pym and Peters seemed to feel this truth. The madman, like the wild beast, appears to need an extraneous stimulus, be it ever so slight, to suggest an initiative: the crooking of a finger, the whispering of a word, may be sufficient, but it must be something. - Ah! Has the moment come? Has the insane man caught some sound inaudible to the others? He pauses. Yes, he is going to act.

"'Oh! friend,' wailed Pym to Peters, in a low voice, 'save her, save her, or where she goes, there go I.'

"Then Peters looks across the chasm, down upon the scene beyond. The opposite brink at this point is ten or twelve feet lower than the spot where Pym and Peters stand, which gives them an excellent view of Lilama and Ahpilus. It is impossible to say just why, but it is obvious that the time which they dread has come. Ahpilus stands looking at the beautiful maiden who crouches in front of him; and as he gazes his powerful form seems to swell, as does that of a wild animal that has determined to spring upon its prey. His arms move forward to grasp her. He has no fear of interruption - he has for the moment forgotten the strangers. He slightly alters his position - his back is toward the chasm - his hands touch the person of his prey. Lilama partly raises her head. She glances past the maniac for a last look at her lover. She does not scream, even as those vise-like hands close upon her, and slowly, oh, so slowly, but steadily, draw her within that iron embrace - slowly, slowly, as might a maniac devotee move in the desecration of his idol.

"But why does she not scream? Why are her eyes fastened - not on her lover - not on the madman, but upon another object? What is that object? Is it a man? Can any man move as that thing moves? Surely that cannot be a man, that streak of drab color - yonder thing that casts to the ground a garment, then shoots backward twenty feet from the abyss - swifter than a panther, as silent as death, with two balls of living fire glaring from - from a face? Surely not a human face! Yes, it is a human face. She does not see the pallid face, the wild eyes of her lover, looking, too, at that thing - that human embodiment of animal agility. No: she has not time to look, for though the human eye is quick, that thing is quicker; and if she take her eye from it for half a second, her gaze will lose it. She cannot take from it her gaze - she is fascinated. Within the past second of time an heroic resolve has been formed, and a drama has begun; in the next two seconds an act in the drama will be completed; in sixty seconds more, a whole tragedy will be added to the list of human sorrows.

"No tongue can tell what cannot quite be seen. A rush of color toward that awful gap; it reaches the edge; it rises in the air and shoots out over that gulf that might indeed have been the portal of Tartarus. Fifty feet as flies the bird. It is in the air - it is half-way over - and yet the maniac has seen it not. But the maniac is turning with his victim in his arms. The streak of drab has passed forty feet - ten feet further if it is to reach the other brink - ten thousand if it fails to reach it; and it has already sunk ten feet in space - with ten feet more of horizontal distance to cover, it is already on a level with the edge of the abyss which it must safely reach, or - The maniac has turned; and the streak of drab has reached the brink - but, ah! below the surface. The form is that of Peters - the only man who could be in such a situation yet live on. One of those invincible arms is thrown upon the surface above the chasm, and those long fingers fasten upon the immovable lava. And now the madman sees the danger that menaces his design - but too late, for Peters the unconquerable stands erect between him and the chasm. Then Ahpilus quickly sets on the ground his living burden; and Peters, the human bird of passage, risks again his life.

"But, for a man like Peters, such a contest was scarcely a risk. Had Ahpilus been less savage in his baffled rage, Peters would have spared the madman; but it was not to be. There was scarcely a man in all Hili-li that could physically cope with Ahpilus; but he was no match for Peters. For a few moments the sailor protected himself without any act of aggression; but

Charles Romyn Dake

it soon became apparent that he would be obliged to destroy his adversary, or himself be destroyed. Ahpilus had pushed Peters, or Peters had carelessly allowed himself to shift his own position, to within dangerously close proximity to the chasm. and at the moment when Peters noticed this circumstance, he also saw that he was between Ahpilus and the abyss: and Ahpilus, in all his furious madness, also observed his advantage. Peters had in his possession a very long and keen knife, but, as he afterward said in talking over this incident, he had never yet seen the time when he was compelled to use an artificial weapon in an encounter with a single combatant; and particularly would he never have used a knife, even though his adversary were a maniac, if a maniac without an artificial weapon. Peters saw that Diregus had found Pym, and, as was also the boatman, he and Pym were, of course, viewing the struggle. I should not, however, have included Pym in the party of observers; for he knew too well how the combat would end to be much absorbed in it. He had no eyes for anything but Lilama. - But to return: As Ahpilus saw his advantage, by a supreme effort he summoned all his great muscular strength, and aided by that invincible motor, the will of a madman, he endeavored to force Peters over the brink. At that precise moment the sailor had his right hand closed on the top of Ahpilus's left shoulder. and his left hand just beneath Ahpilus's right arm on the side of the exile's chest. He quickly shifted his left hand to the side of the hip; and then those great gorilla arms raised from the ground the body of the madman, swung it overhead as another man might swing the body of a three-year-old child, as he did so bringing the back of his adversary downward; and then came a movement of Herculean power in which the long arms approximated with a twisting, bending effect; two vertebras in Ahpilus's back at the point of least resistance separated, the spine was dislocated, and a mass of helpless, vibrating human flesh fell at the feet of the victor. Peters, whilst his brute instinct was in full possession of him, might, instead of dropping Ahpilus to the ground, have thrown the body into the abyss; but Diregus had anticipated such an action, and called to Peters not to injure the poor insane fellow more than was necessary to prevent him from injuring others. Ahpilus was not dead - that is, he was not dead over his entire body: the hips and all below were as nerveless as the body of a corpse; but above the hips, the same old vigor remained - and so it would be though he lived for yet a hundred years."

Here Doctor Bainbridge ceased to speak. Doctor Castleton had entered the room two or three minutes before, and, keeping silent, had heard the last three or four hundred words, which described the close of that brief but terrible combat.

THE FIFTEENTH CHAPTER

"Well," said Doctor Castleton, as Bainbridge closed. "Peters could, when he was fifty years younger, have done that very thing to any living man weighing not more than a hundred and eighty or a hundred and ninety pounds. I myself have seen him throw to the ground a powerful horse, and the little giant must have been older than sixty at the time. Then again, he possesses that wonderful instinct of certainty in action which belongs to purely animal life. It is said that the tiger when it strikes never misses its aim; and that our American panther makes the most unusual leaps without ever making an attempt beyond its powers. I have many times observed that even our comparatively degenerate domestic cat very rarely indeed, if ever, fails to accomplish the purpose of a stroke. Peters possesses, or did possess, that instinct."

"Yes," said Bainbridge, "you are right. Peters says that on almost every vessel he ever shipped on he was called 'the baboon' - because of his great physical power and agility, he says; but as we know, rather because of his extremely short stature, his large mouth - in fact, his resemblance in many striking ways to the gorilla, or the orang-outang; and perhaps, also, in part, to his habit, mentioned in Pym's description of him, of feigning mental aberration - assuming to be 'simple.'"

"This won't do," said Castleton, with that peculiar look on his face which always appeared when he was about to deflect from the serious to the humorous. "Whilst I should not object to hearing my old friend Peters called a gorilla, I draw the line at gorilla. I should object to the appellation orang-outang, and I should resent with emphasis that of baboon. But gorilla I will accept, for in many ways the gorilla is, or at least once was, the superior of man. Even if we limit the source of our deductions to the skeleton of the animal, the truth of my last assertion is strongly evidenced. In the first place, the gorilla is more sedate and less pettily curious than man; this is proved by his having only three, instead of four, bones in the last division of his spine, giving him a shorter caudal appendage than man's, and proving the animal to be farther from the monkey than are we; then in the second place, the gorilla has thirteen ribs, which would seem to be rational evidence that, whatever the present gorilla may be, his ancestors of by-gone ages were handsomer than man; because in the gorilla's first search for a wife the field of operations was not limited to his own chest."

"That will do very well, doctor; but don't you think you are a little severe on Adam?" I said.

"I have no sympathies with Adam. Not that I ever blamed him for his weakness in the apple incident; but I do blame him for his garrulity, and his paltry cowardice in exposing Eve. Eve was an instinctive agnostic - and she didn't purpose to be anybody's slave. If Adam decided to keep up with the procession, as he at first did decide to do, he had no business to whine over the outcome. I'd wager freely that Eve earned the living after the pair left paradise. Cain took after his mother; and I hazard the opinion that Eve was in sympathy with Cain in the Abel episode - that is, after the tragedy. Eve and Cain had the best of everything all the way through, for they acted in harmony with their feelings; whilst poor old feeble, vacillating Adam tried to use his worthless old brain-box, and the natural consequence ensued. His feelings, which constituted the strongest part of his mind, were always in conflict with his intellect, which was just strong enough to get him into trouble when a pure out-and-out unreasoning animal would have been safe; and he never had enough will properly to correct an error when he did see it."

Charles Romyn Dake

We laughed over this conceit of Castleton's, and Bainbridge said:

"Speaking of biblical characters, I have thought that Moses would, with even slight literary training, have far surpassed the modern writer of adventure-fiction. His style may be open to adverse criticism, but his originality is beyond question. If he left any material for a purely original story, I fail to detect it. He gave to literature the sea-story, the war-story, and the love-story - stories that hinge on all the human passions, and stories of the supernatural in all its phases. He first presented to a world innocent of fiction-literature the giant and the dwarf; the brave man, the strong man, and the man of supreme fortitude; the honest man, the truthful king, and the woman that knows how to wait for the man she loves; voices in the air, signs in the sky - in short, everything. Even poor old Aesop wasn't in time to grasp a reputation for originality. The modern story-teller may combine, extend, and elaborate; but all opportunity for a display of invention seems to be forever barred."

"By the bye, doctor," said Castleton, evidently impatient at his enforced silence whilst another spoke, "do any of your volcanoes or mountains in Hili-li blow up?"

"No, sir," answered Bainbridge, with dignity.

"Well, if I had been Pym I should have blown those mountains into the Antarctic Ocean," said Castleton. "I understand from the words that I caught this evening as I entered here that your heroine is safe; but if I had been Pym, I should have taken no risks. I should have sent your madman word to return the girl, or take the consequences - the consequences being that I should have blown him and the entire mountain into the mighty deep. 'Sir,' I should have said, 'return the lady, or I will annihilate you.' And so I should have done, if a hair of her head had been harmed. - By the bye, gentlemen, I believe you never heard of my invention for stopping war, did you?" We intimated that we had thus far been deprived of that pleasure. I saw that one of his peculiar outbursts was at hand - one of those apparently serious, though, I thought, intentionally humorous sallies, so puzzling coming from a man of Castleton's intellectual attainments, and the mental *primum mobile* of which I had already been much interested in trying to determine.

"Well, gentlemen," he continued, "it was about fourteen years ago, during the dark days of The War" - he referred to the great rebellion in the United States, which began in 1861, and which it required the existing government about four years to suppress. "It was during the period when our great President was most worried. I had thought the matter over - as I always do think over vast questions, from the standpoint of true greatness. 'Why not,' I mentally soliloquized, 'why not end this matter at a blow? 'As I drove about through our retired roads and lanes, I gave the subject my very best attention. I thought to myself how the present system of the universe depends upon what we term the luminiferous ether; of the perfect elasticity and inexpansibility of that ether; of what its nature must be. I concluded that no ultimate particle of it - as with matter no atom - is ever added to or removed from the universe. Now, if we could succeed in removing from this inexpansible, universal ocean of ether even the most ultimate portion, there would be a literal vacuum with nothing to fill it, and the equilibrium of the universe would be destroyed. Now, gentlemen, is or is not this supposition logical?"

We admitted our inability to deny its truth.

"'Well, then,' I reasoned, looking at the subject on the reverse side, 'could an additional portion of ether be created, there would be in space no place to receive it; the universe in its present state - a state in which what we term matter or substance exists - would just simply cease to exist - instantly, and within the compass of every star and planet.'

"But how to create that particle of ether - that was what occupied my mind for weeks. I would seem to grasp the hint that came and went within the recesses of a brain which - so say my friends - has perhaps never had its equal for variety of conception and rapid response to the slightest external or internal stimulus. Now, many physicists suppose matter to be simply a form of ether - plainly, that matter originated out of ether - was made from ether; so that, after all, the universe was created from nothing - that is, nothing if we correctly define matter. It was but a step for me, then, to the end: remove all radiant energy from a fixed gas - a gas without the property of condensation to another form of matter, *i.e.*, to a fluid or a solid - and the thing, I said to myself, is done. I am positive that I know of such a gas, and within a few years all physicists will recognize it. At present the method of procuring it is my secret, as I may still wish to experiment with what is now but a theoretical discovery, though certain to unfold in practice exactly as I have explained it. You understand, of course, that I remove from my gas, by artificial cold and compression, the last vestige of heat, my gas becomes ether, there is no place for it in the universal ocean of inexpansible ether, the balance of the universe as it now exists is destroyed, all matter instantly ceases to exist, and we just sit back and wait for a few billions of trillions of cycles of time, until another system of nature is formed."

For a time we all kept silence: Doctor Bainbridge, I suppose, like myself, marvelling at the peculiarities of our strange companion. At last I said:

"And how about the war, doctor?"

"Now comes the humiliation!" he replied. "Oh, must genius ever grovel at the feet of mere physical power - insolent official power! Why are great men so difficult of access! Why, in 1453, did not Constantine in his day of trouble listen to your brainy countryman, and save Europe from the inroads of the Turk? Well, I hastened to Washington City, determined that no ear other than the President's own should hear the secret; and that no power on earth should draw it from me. I went to the White House. I admit that war-times are busy times - but those infernal White House flunkies kept me waiting in the reception-rooms for four hours! I told my plans to the ushers, to a waiting soldier or two, and to a foreign diplomat with whom I struck up a talk. All of them acted suspiciously, and I believe were jealous of my wisdom. When, for the third time, an usher took my card - or pretended to take my card - to the President, his secretary came down to me. At first I told him that my secret was for the President's ear alone; but at last I gave him a clew to the nature of my business. He left me, but he did not return. Such is reflected political power. But I thought of my power - aye, and physical power, too - the only real power. I never blamed the President - I to this day believe that that fellow H - never told Lincoln of my visit to the White House."

After an appreciative murmur and movement on the part of Bainbridge and myself - for we felt like laughing, and yet sighs of wonderment were expected by Castleton - and after a grunt from Arthur in his corner, I asked, for want of something better to say,

"Were you ever in the army, doctor?"

"Well - ah - no - yes - no, sir; not exactly," Castleton replied. "But I had a younger brother who beat the drum for a whole week in an enlisting-office tent in Chicago. Poor boy! he died of brain fever in 1869 - always a genius - great brain. - And this talk reminds me that I am getting no pension from the United States Government on that poor, neglected, sacrificed boy. Curse my thoughtlessness! Yes, and - but no: I belong to the old school of patriots - I will not curse my country."

As Castleton uttered the last sentence, he approached the door of exit to the hall. He had as usual been pacing the floor; and with the closing word he shot into the hall and was gone. And as the sound of his footsteps rang through the corridors of the hotel, Arthur remarked, from his corner:

Charles Romyn Dake

"It's a pity he didn't sit down on his boomerang infernal-machine, and then set it a-going: he might a been on the moon by this time, where the fool belongs, with the other lunatics. If he ever comes into my new ice-cream parlor - (twelve by sixteen, gas-lights, three tables, and six chairs; two spoons furnished with one saucer if desired, and a napkin for your lady free; ten cents a saucer, and ginger-bread thrown in) - why out he goes, too quick. Oh, he's a daisy, he is! If you ever want to remind me of him, anybody, ask me to lend you a dime; and when I shake my head and my teeth rattle, I'll remember the lunkhead, sure enough."

I frowned down the youngster, for he had promised not to obtrude his opinion in the presence of Bainbridge. But as his words did not refer in any manner to the story that Bainbridge was telling us, I should not have objected to them, but that with Arthur it was necessary to be cautious in creating precedents, which, as I have intimated, in his case almost immediately congealed into vested rights; and our agreement had obligated him to observe complete silence on the subject of Peters' story, and, if I correctly remember - though Arthur denied this latter - on all other subjects, in the presence of Doctor Bainbridge.

As Bainbridge appeared to have nothing further to say, and was making those slight occasional movements which I knew presaged his departure, I began to talk of Peters' leap; and in the most guarded manner - for with Bainbridge any question of the facts of his narrative required tact and delicacy to avoid the giving of offence - to discuss the subject of leaping in general, the facts and probabilities relating to distance, and the laws and conditions that might govern and regulate the running-leap.

"Do you not think," I finally asked, "that Peters somewhat overestimates the distance of his marvelous leap? I am aware that Peters was, both in strength and in agility, almost preter-human; but fifty feet or thereabouts! That seems scarcely possible. Our best athletes, I believe, have never, on level ground, made a running leap of much more than half that distance. Now forty feet, under all the circumstances, would not strike me as impossible, though thirty-five would better chime with my ideas of the probable, and thirty would remove all possibility of any draft on my credulity."

"It is not a question of ideas or of credulity," answered Bainbridge, "but one of fact. However, we will look at the incident from the stand-point of reason and experience. Now let us assume that a running leap of twenty-five feet on level ground would not be beyond the ability of a trained athlete. I think you will allow to Peters a natural advantage of seven feet over an ordinary athlete, when you consider the superiority of his form, so well adapted to leaping - a form that gives to him the advantage of an orang-outang, without the disadvantage of hand-like feet, so poorly suited to flat surfaces. From the fullest information I could obtain from Peters, I believe that in leaping he obtains more impetus from his arms than from his legs; but even with his preternatural strength he does not get quite as much impulse-force from his legs as would an ordinary athlete. I myself think that the use of his arms in making this leap gave him an advantage of one-third over another man of equal strength. However, I ask you to allow him from all advantage of form, in the leap alone, seven feet, or twenty-eight per cent."

To this proposition I assented.

"Then," continued Bainbridge, "it must be remembered that so far as the actual leap is concerned, he missed the opposite edge of the abyss - for he did miss it, and any other man would have gone to the bottom of the chasm. It was only the length of his arm, with its excessive strength, and the iron grip of that enormous hand, which prevented complete failure. As a matter of fact, the walls of the abyss being fifty feet apart, Peters leaped only forty-seven feet. Am I correct?"

Again I assented.

Charles Romyn Dake

"Then," said Bainbridge, "we have brought within the limits of reason thirty-five of the fifty feet, and fifteen feet remain to be accounted for. Now let us recall to your memory the fact that the edge of the abyss toward which he leaped was twelve feet lower than the edge from which he sprung; and that, in his progress across the chasm he fell, in addition to this twelve feet, his own height - which, according to Pym's diary was, at that period, four feet and eight inches. If Peters could have covered thirty-five feet on level ground, could he have covered fifty feet with the advantage of a drop of nearly seventeen feet? Assuming a certain weight for Peters, we could calculate the number of foot-pounds of energy, or the initial velocity, necessary to make a leap of thirty-five feet on level ground, and how many foot-pounds it would require to make a leap of fifty feet with a drop of sixteen feet and eight inches taken into the conditions. But as most of the equations in our calculation are approximative, I prefer that the element of gravitation should be handled in a general way. If a leaper were to impel himself horizontally only, he would, in the shortest leap, fall below a level. This fall may be met to the extent of about two feet, by drawing up the legs - that is, by 'hunkering' as the leap progresses, and alighting on his feet with the body to that extent lower than when the spring began. In a leap of twenty-five feet, however, the leaper is compelled to project himself upward as well as forward; and an instinctive sense of just how little energy may be expended in raising himself, and how much may be left for the forward impulse, is one of the chief elements of his proficiency. Peters did not have to raise his body at all."

"I begin to comprehend," said I.

"Yes," replied Bainbridge, "the more you think of it, the more convinced will you become that Peters made the leap as he states. Of course he could not have sprung fifty feet, or even forty feet, on a level; for, in a leap of only forty feet, one would have to raise himself more than twelve feet into the air, and (except for a possible small advantage of position in leaping) it requires the same amount of force to raise a body ten feet on an incline, as it does to raise the same body ten feet perpendicularly into space - an impossible feat, even to Peters at twenty-eight or thirty years of age."

"I quite believe that he did it," I said, "and when we consider that he claims to have measured the distance only mentally, and that he might therefore honestly have mistaken it to the extent of a few feet, I am willing to say that my confidence in his intended veracity is unshaken - even if he is an old sailor."

"Yes," said Bainbridge, "and we must not overlook the fact that a man's mental state at the time of performing a physical feat is a very important determining factor in the result of the performance. A powerful but lackadaisical fellow might, with only a few dollars at stake, make a very poor showing; yet to preserve his life he might make a really wonderful leap. What effect, then, did mental condition exert on a man like Peters under the circumstances attending this unparalleled leap? Think of the enormous muscular power developed by the message received through the nerves from a mind thus affected! His own life, and that of another, if not of two others, depended upon the success of his effort. Under such circumstances muscular power would either be paralyzed, or else intensified beyond our common conception of such force. Peters positively asserts, that when a boy of sixteen he frequently leaped from the flat upper deck of a boat - that is, from a height of twenty feet - into the surrounding water, habitually covering a distance of from forty to forty-five feet; whilst other boys, under the same conditions, rarely covered twenty-five feet, and never thirty."

A moment later Bainbridge arose to depart; but he lingered for a moment, standing, and with his left hand resting on the centre table, began to speak in a general way of the great antarctic crater and its surrounding wonders. It was my habit to make full notes of the actual facts stated by him in the more formal parts of these evening recitals, and sometimes even of his comments; and I regret that I did not do so at the particular moment to which I am now alluding. It was not until the following morning that I made a few memoranda of the closing incident of the evening. With the help of these notes and a fairly good memory, I hope to be able at this late day to describe for the reader an episode that I should dislike entirely to omit from this narrative.

He spoke for several minutes of the wonderful power of nature to accomplish certain ends - the force that accomplishes which, he termed a *purpose* in nature; and he made some remarks along the line of a contention, that the development of all matter into higher forms was what he called an unconscious intention, explaining that there was no paradox in the expression "unconscious intention"; for, he said, even men, individual men, are constantly performing a thousand acts that have an unconscious purpose or intention - as, for instance, the automatic action of winding a watch without the slightest exercise of will, and without remembering the action. This unconscious motive-force, he said, is inherent in vegetables as well as in animals, and that in fact it exists, though relatively of very slow and feeble action, in all matter, the power being an attribute of all molecules, and even of elemental atoms. He, however, claimed no originality for any of the views which he expressed.

"To my consciousness," he said, "the conviction of individual immortality is so clear that, if I were not perfectly aware of the cause of their doubt or disbelief, I should wonder at intelligent persons questioning the fact. Like everything else taught by Christ, that we are immortal is a fact; and it is not in a billion years that we shall live again under new conditions, but, as He intimated, 'to-morrow.' And I surmise that we shall not do so in any absurdly physical way, nor yet in a manner so deeply abstruse that it would require a logician and a professional physicist, were it explained, to comprehend it. As with all that God has given us, we shall find the conditions of the next life very simple. Educated men - nearly all highly educated men, and particularly educated theologians - when they touch this subject remind me of the cuttle-fish. There is nothing around them that is not perfectly transparent until, by their own act, everything is obscured to themselves and to their neighbors. But whilst the cuttle-fish swims out of the zone of opacity created by himself, the theologian remains in his, fighting the obscurity with logic - for that purpose the poorest of all devices. You cannot guide an emotional boat with an intellectual rudder. Something to me much more convincing than reason, tells me that our bodies will not be long in their graves before we shall again begin to live; and my feeling is, that, though consciousness will at the death of this body be obscured for a time, it will not be lost for a *long* time. I feel that almost at once after death the mystery of conscious individuality will again assert itself. Refined by this life, as the molecular construction of inorganic matter is refined by passing through organic life, so the consciousness lately within the molecules of your discarded body, will not be as the consciousness within like molecules of mineral or of vegetable matter; for it will be your consciousness - *your* consciousness, created by God and developed by His edict - developed after slumbering for ages within the mineral; awakening to quicker action in the vegetable world; touching the domain of conscious memory in lower animals; aroused to keener moral and intellectual existence in your late body, and at last made ready for a new mystery - what, we know not - in another world, possibly in the direction of what we might call a 'fourth dimension' of consciousness. Oh, no; there should not be anything to prevent us from knowing now that we shall continue to exist, and to go ever upward, upward, upward. Nature permits us, in each sphere of being, to catch a glimpse of the succeeding one, if only we will not ourselves obstruct the view."

A moment later he dropped into an animated, almost rhapsodical, running comment on some of the scenic beauties surrounding Hili-li.

"Imagine," he said, "what the scenic effects must have been, everywhere within the illumination of that great lake of fire, covering an area of nearly two hundred square miles - that great lake of white, boiling, earthy matter, brilliantly lighting the long antarctic night. Think of those mountains, with the Olympian offshoot six miles in height; and of the peak called Mount Olympus, looming up ten thousand feet above even that great mountain-range. Try to picture the valleys, the chasms, the overhanging cliffs, the many smaller active craters, like mammoth watch-fires lighted on the mountain-tops in all directions; and the masses of glistening salt, thrown by upheavals of the earth high upon the mountain-side. Cannot you almost behold the scene? May we not, with the brush of fancy, paint for our mental vision many a strange, weird picture? Here we see, high on the mountain-front, a mass of crystal salt - many millions of tons - thrown, by a mere fillip of terrestrial power, thirty thousand feet above the ocean level, to rest and sparkle like a gem on the bosom of that old mountain-god, Olympus. Then, still higher, on the very summit - for even here, in the glare of this great crater, where evaporation rains upward from the sea, all vapor is quickly condensed and frozen on the higher peaks - we see, like the tresses of the aged, the pearly snow and ice overhanging the Olympian brow. Aye, may we not even -"

Well, dear reader, I expect to be censured. As Bainbridge drew toward what I suppose would, under any circumstances, have been his close, I was sitting with my face toward Arthur, and the actions of that unpolished gem told me that the catastrophe was at hand. Those who say that "the expected never happens" misinform us; for the expected very frequently does happen. The wretched boy did not - would not - look at me, and I could not, of course, interrupt the flow of eloquence that poured from the lips of Bainbridge. What could I have done? Even at this late day, I cannot see what I could have done, though I did know the nature of what was coming. It was the words "snow and ice" that added the last straw which broke the camel's back, and let fall the load of annoyance; and as Bainbridge uttered the words, "Aye, may we not even -," Arthur, that miserable factotum, whom I had so rashly trusted, shot from his chair into the air; and, with arms waving, and eyes glistening with excitement, he fairly yelled:

"Great geewhilikin! Think of that ice, and that salt, and that climate! Now if a fellow only had a drove of Giganticus cows, with old Olympus for 'em to run over free, where would the other ice-cream fellows be? Free ice, free salt, free cream, free fodder, and no end of 'em all, too! Why, in that hot hole a man 'ud be a ice-cream king in no time. Well, now! doesn't that make your windows bulge? You're a shoutin', Doc. Please don't speak again in the same language till I rest my mind, if you love me!"

I could not stop him. Frowning had no effect, and toward the end of his outburst I even protested in words. But it was no use. He spoke quickly, and he spoke very loudly, and not a word was lost on Bainbridge. Bainbridge had a fine sense of humor; but like many other humorists, he did not relish jocosities of which he was the subject. Any levity in any manner connected with Hili-li, I knew would be to him unendurable. He had from the beginning taken the Peters disclosures, and even the old sailor himself, very seriously. Little happenings during our stay at the old sailor's home, which had brought a smile to my own face, had never for a moment altered the countenance of Bainbridge from the stern seriousness becoming that of one who is gathering facts of the most solemn import. I am positive that he would have taken with a poor grace the slightest levity from even myself on the subject of Hili-li. But from the bell-boy of a hotel! Olympus to become a pasture field for mastodon cows! Its ice and its saline wonders to be employed in the making of ice-cream!

Well, I just sat, and said nothing, and blamed myself. The thing was done, as it is said, and could not be undone. Doctor Bainbridge looked at me, with an injured but resigned expression, which seemed to say. "Well, you see you've done it; you *would* allow the creature to drink in the nectar of refined literary production, and one of the natural results has followed." He took up his hat, and more in grief than in anger, he made his adieux, and quietly walked out of the doorway, through the hallway, down the stairs, and out of the house. And a moment later I said:

"Now, young man, you probably see what you have done! We may, or we may not hear more of Lilama, of Pym, of Ahpilus, and the others. I am anxious to know what became of the poor fellow, Ahpilus; and I intend to find out, if I have to go to Peters for the information." Then, as I saw the boy was really repentant; and when I began to consider the fact that he could not comprehend why Bainbridge should be offended, when no offence had been intended, I mentally threw all the blame upon myself, and added:

"But never mind; it does not amount to much. Doctor Bainbridge will probably be here to-morrow evening, and will, no doubt, have forgotten, or at least buried the incident. But after this, Arthur, you may come to me each morning, and as I dress I will tell you all about what the evening before I shall learn from the doctor. So, goodnight to you, and here is a dollar to help you start the ice-cream parlor."

THE SIXTEENTH CHAPTER

On the following evening, at his usual hour, Bainbridge entered my apartment; and after the customary greeting, seated himself. No mention was made of Arthur's hapless interruption of the evening before, Bainbridge acting as if that miserable incident had not occurred.

"If I remember rightly," he said, "we left Ahpilus lying with a broken back, and Peters standing by him, with Lilama crouching near; whilst on the opposite side of the chasm or canyon stood Pym, Diregus, and the boatman, who had accompanied the rescue party in their ascent of the mountain.

"After a moment of astonishment, Diregus inquired concerning the condition of Ahpilus; and Peters replied that the maniac not only lived, but was not in danger of dying; that he was scarcely conscious, however, and that even if fully aroused would in all probability not be able to walk - Peters knowing from personal experience with similar 'accidents' what the results were likely to be.

"When Lilama heard Peters' statement, she approached the injured man - the friend of her childhood and her girlhood - and did what little she could to make his position at least appear more comfortable.

"There was no possible way for the divided party to unite, other than by returning several miles down the mountain-side. Now that Lilama was safe, and Ahpilus not only mentally alienated from his people but also physically helpless, a kindly feeling came to the party for their old friend thus reduced to a condition doubly lamentable, and very pitiable to persons so refined and sensitive as were the Hili-lites. There was some discussion on the subject of Ahpilus's future; and then Peters said that he could easily carry the injured man down the mountain-side. This he at once began to do; and in the course of four or five hours, during which he stopped for a rest a number of times, he reached a point in the descent at which the canyon narrowed to a width of not more than ten feet, and across which a rude foot-bridge of logs had been constructed. Lilama, as well as those on the opposite side of the chasm, had kept pace with Peters; and the divided party now came together.

"Ahpilus was gently placed on the ground; and as his old friends gathered about him it was observed that not only had consciousness returned, but that the helpless man looked quite the Ahpilus of former and happier days. As his old friends looked into his eyes, those windows of the mind, they saw a soul unruffled, and at peace with nature.

"Then Diregus addressed to Ahpilus some words of inquiry; but it was soon apparent that the stricken man could answer no question relating to recent days, or even to the past year or two. In fact, Diregus soon recognized that Ahpilus knew nothing of his own past from a period antedating his exile to the present time. It appears that the nervous shock which accompanied the breaking of his spine had, in some way, dispelled his madness, and also those less maniacal, comparatively mild delusions which for several years had clouded and perverted his otherwise brilliant mind; so that he was again the same loving and lovable Ahpilus of former times; but in all the sixty or seventy years that he might yet live, he never again would be able to walk, or even to stand, unaided.

"The party of five, carrying the helpless man, sadly and silently continued on their way to Volcano Bay, which in the course of an hour they reached. There they found the other boatmen waiting for them, and, also, standing here and there in groups, a number of the exiles, among them Medosus. It had gone forth among these pariahs of Hili-liland, that something unusual was astir; and, fearing something, they knew not what, they had determined to observe the movements of the invading party. Diregus soon explained what had brought them to Olympus, and the results of their search. The exiles were at first quite unable to believe that Peters had crossed the chasm at the point stated, though lying was in Hili-li a lost art, the history of that country stating positively that but three adult liars (visitors excepted) had existed in Hili-li for five hundred years, the last of whom had, two centuries before, died. When the Olympians (as the exiles were generally in derision called) learned of Ahpilus's condition, and of its cause, it appeared for a few moments that Peters would be attacked; but the soothing words of Pym and Diregus, and the presence of Lilama, whom they knew had been in extreme danger, as well as the expression on the face of Peters when he first grasped the idea that an attack upon him was imminent - all of these things together prevented trouble.

"When the party had made Ahpilus as comfortable as possible in the bottom of the boat, and had seated themselves preparatory to their return, Medosus stepped down to the shore, and asked Diregus if he would convey for the exiles a message to the King and Councillors of Hili-li, and also to the aged mystic, Masusaelili, who, though not an official, was in reality the chief adviser of those who did control the kingdom. Diregus, whose father was perhaps second only to the King - it was supposed by many that the Duke was the real power behind the throne, and it was within the range of reasonable possibility that his son, Diregus, might some day reign - replied that he must hear the message before making any promise. Then Medosus, knowing that his former friend and schoolmate was at heart in sympathy with the exiles, and did not really believe them to be in any way vicious (Diregus himself had twice offended, as had a majority of all Hili-lite youths, past and present; but he had not offended for a third time), spoke as follows:

Charles Romyn Dake

"'Say for us to His Majesty, and to the Honorable Councillors, that we, the so-called Exiles of Olympus, request our release, and also permission to return to Hili-li. In making this request we are not willing to say that we have ever in the past done to the State any serious wrong. We have, however, reached a time of life when we are willing to abjure the delights and benefits of wrestling, of ground-ball, of bat-ball, and of other athletic sports. We are willing to promise not again to visit the savages of surrounding islands - a rare sport. We regret the broken neck of young Selimus, which occurred during a game of ground-ball some three years ago, and we regret the accidental breaking of a few other bones; but we think these accidents no more deplorable than the death of Testube the scholar, or the blinding of the chemist, Amurosus - accidents which occurred whilst they were in their own laboratories, performing experiments of no material benefit, so far as we know, to the people of Hili-li. I might also allude to the lamentable death of Solarsistus, who some four years ago fell from his tower whilst observing the noted shower of falling meteors. And we ask these wise men - particularly Masusaelili, whose mind is as cultivated as his body is neglected - what they think would become of the people of Hili-li if, at some future time, even so few as one thousand such men as these two strangers standing there should make war upon us, assuming that the decrees of those in power shall have been for a single generation faithfully observed. When the barbarian of the north overcame our ancestors in ancient Rome, it was only after indolent habits had sapped the physical power of the patrician; and when we here repelled with ease many times our number of barbarians, it was whilst yet our race was hardy from its combat with adverse forces in this then new land. We have not forgotten the strange power which Masusaelili is able to exert over a limited number of persons at one time. We are not unaware of the beneficent results of those laws and customs that compel the most of our people, between the ages of eighteen and fifty, to perform physical labor during twelve hours of each week; but we maintain that the elements of contest and danger are necessary concomitants of physical exertion, if we are to acquire and retain the manly quality of physical bravery, and that other quality so frequently wanting in him who is only a scholar - fortitude.

"'Look,' he continued, pointing to Peters. 'There stands a man inured to physical danger. A few hours ago he was placed where prompt resolution was demanded to decide the fate of one of the loveliest creatures upon whom the light of yonder crater-fire ever shone - perhaps upon whom the sun ever shone; he had scarcely sixty seconds of time in which to determine whether she should die, or he should take the chance of a terrible death, with a hand-to-hand conflict, a powerful madman for an adversary, certain to confront him should his leap by a miracle prove successful. To have leaped over an abyss of half the width of that one, and then to have met an ordinary adversary, would have been a wonderfully brave deed. He decided promptly - and, too, he succeeded. No man in Hili-li could have done half as much, even had he dared attempt the feat.

"'That, I think, is all,' continued Medosus. 'We have rarely found our rulers deaf to reasonable petitions, and we believe that they will, upon mature deliberation, annul our sentences of ten years' banishment. If I do not overtax your time and your patience, I should like to ask you, Diregus, to suggest to your father and to Masusaelili this thought: Since the termination of those extended surveys which the State inaugurated and terminated after the departure of that ship which visited us about two hundred and fifty years ago, we have been aware that Hili-li is situated in a great inland sea, about twelve hundred miles in diameter, which sea contains from two hundred to three hundred islands, and in which our main island occupies a position some three hundred miles from the nearest mainland in one direction, and some nine hundred miles from the nearest mainland in another direction. We are also aware that the sailing vessel which came to us found an entrance through this vast ring-like continent, which entrance-way is only three hundred miles in width, and is the only means of access to this inland sea, except a narrower channel diametrically opposite to the broader one. The broader opening, in its main part, is traversed by warm currents outward, which remain warm until the continent is passed; and by one broad central warm current inward, which is very swift, and the source of the great warmth of which we have never been able to determine. The narrower passage, generally completely frozen, or choked with ice, conveys to the central sea only water at nearly the freezing temperature. The mainland consists chiefly of volcanic mountains, is apparently covered with ice, and is wholly impassable. Now, we have long thought ourselves safe from the outer world, as we really are from the savages of the other islands within this great sea. We know that in the first thousand years of our history there came to us once two wrecked sailors, and at another time a single sailor; then came the ship; and since then every ten to thirty years we have had some token, animate or inanimate, from the great beyond. But none that came, save the ship-load of two hundred and fifty years ago, ever left us; and those who sailed that vessel could not again have found us, had they tried during the remainder of their lives. Hence, our Councillors appear to think that we shall forever remain secreted here in safety. Now I only wish to suggest to those who are wiser, but whose minds are not like ours sharpened by hardship and solitude, that some great event in the vast outer world must have occurred preceding the visit of that ship. The conditions of the world have in some manner changed. Yet, whilst the vast ring-like continent of ice-covered volcanoes will long protect us, the warm strait will be discovered and mapped, and then design will carry to us many, over the same course by which chance has conveyed a few. As usual, I suppose, these two men will not be allowed to leave us. But in some way the outside world will learn of us and of our exhaustless supplies of these pebbles' (he pointed to nuggets of gold lying on the shore of the bay), 'which we know are the same as others in our museum, that our ancestors brought from Rome, and of which - so says our ancient history - one pebble the size of a fingerend would purchase a human captive! Some chance will carry to those people (no doubt the descendants of those barbarians who almost exterminated our Roman ancestors) a knowledge of this.' Here Medosus picked from the ground a nugget of gold about the size of a large orange, and threw it carelessly from him into the bay. 'Aurum,' he said, disdainfully; 'aurum, the curse of our ancestors! What would not the outer world endure to gain the ship-loads of this stuff that lie scattered over our volcanic islands? Stuff which we use only in building and for pavements, because it is easily worked, and bright, and lasting. What will our people do when ship-loads of men like these two strangers come to us? And, come, too, not almost starved and without weapons, but with spears, and practised arms to use their spears. Astuteness is a poor weapon, when it is the only weapon, against men who are maddened with avarice: bravery, physical power, fortitude; the strong arm, backed by the quick eye, and the mind inured to danger - these, in such a time of need, will alone avail to protect our lives, our land, and our homes from a ruthless foe.

"'Pardon my prolixity; but, as I talked, I became more interested in the fate of my countrymen, even than in that of my fellow-exiles and myself. You understand me, my old friend? I know that you will speak for us. Good-by.'

"And then wishing the exiles good-by, the party in the boat moved from the shore - at first by paddle-power; but on reaching the outlet of Volcano Bay the sails of their boat were spread for the run across the open sea."

Here Doctor Bainbridge paused for a moment in his narration, lighted a cigar, took a whiff or two, and then continued:

"You must pardon me for entering so fully into the affairs of Medosus and his fellow-exiles. It was only by tact and patience that, little by little, I gathered from Peters the facts. My excuse for this verbosity is, that from the speech of Medosus - whose words show that he supposed Pym and Peters would never be allowed to leave Hili-li - we obtain, better than from all other sources of information which were opened to Peters, an insight of the geographical knowledge, and of many of the peculiarities, of a strange, isolated people - a people which, beyond all doubt, I think, is descended from the pure imperial

Roman stock; and also because it explains the means by which the exiles afterward obtained their liberty, and were thus enabled to assist their relatives and friends in the City of Hili-li, at a time when, though of brief duration, the islands of Hili-li were threatened with depopulation. It seems that the message of Medosus, joined with the lesson of Lilama's abduction, carrying as it did a suggestion of future possibilities should the exiles continue to increase in number whilst growing more reckless, and at the same time no strangers be at hand to assist in overcoming them - these considerations, and the influence of Pym, who described the quality of English, German, French, and American soldiers that were produced in lands where, he said, sports and games similar to those of Hili-li (he explained the nature of sparring, cricket, etc.) were in no manner restricted by law. (This, you will remember, was in the year 1828.)

"The rescue party were met at the Duke's landing by all the residents of the palace, and by many relatives and friends of Lilama, who had gathered to receive her. As soon as Peters' wonderful feat was explained, he became the hero of the island.

"The Hili-lites showed themselves in one respect much like other races. They had no sooner decided to rescind the interdict against the hitherto obnoxious athletic games, than all classes began to patronize these sports, and immediately they became very popular; and to the other games was added that of contests at leaping. Some of the feats performed at this time by Peters were certainly astonishing. One of his performances which took place during an exhibition in the presence of the elite of Hili-li, was to leap from an improvised platform, placed eighty feet above the ground, grasp the limb of a tree which projected about thirty feet beneath and several feet away from the platform, instantly drop to another limb, twenty-five feet lower, and then to the ground. To an observer he appeared to jump from the platform, to strike one limb and then another in his descent, and to fall, a mass of bruised flesh and broken bones, upon the earth; the real climax being when, instead, he fell lightly on his feet, and walked away to prepare for his next act in this public display.

"But we must hasten on. And before proceeding to subjects of greater interest, I will tell at once what was the future of Ahpilus. He had when a boy been noted for a love of study, and now when he could no longer walk, he turned his attention to literary pursuits. Masusaelili took an interest in the unfortunate young man, and allowed him at first to be brought occasionally to the studio which the reader has already visited, and later to become an assistant in his researches. Peters and Pym felt very kindly to the poor fellow, and evinced their regard by inventing and making for him a sort of chair on two main wheels and a small third wheel, upon which he could sit and guide himself with ease and comfort from place to place in the city, and that, too, with quite as great speed as he had in the past been able to attain by walking. The last thing heard of him by Peters was, that he had begun a history of the Hili-lite people, from the settlement of Hili-li to 1828. And this reminds me to say that, to Pym and Peters, one of the strangest things in Hili-li was their count of time, which appeared the same as our own. It was not in fact the same, however, though Peters insists that it was; for whilst we, of course, count time according to the Gregorian calendar, the Hili-lites must have counted time according to the Julian calendar. This would have placed the Hili-lites about eleven days in arrear of Pym's count - a difference which, under the circumstances, Peters might easily have overlooked.

"Not many weeks after the rescue of Lilania, she and Pym were married according to the usual form of Hili-li. The wedding ceremony was a very quiet one. I have thought that perhaps the customs of Hili-li might account for the lack of any festivity; and, again, that the Ahpilus incident may have precluded all social gaiety at such a time, the injured man being still in a precarious condition."

Here Bainbridge paused for a moment, took a turn or two across the floor, relit the long-neglected cigar that he held in his fingers, seated himself, and continued:

Charles Romyn Dake

THE SEVENTEENTH CHAPTER

It is pleasant to dwell on this period in the life of young Pym.
We think of his home on the far-away island of Nantucket,
with the loving mother, the proud father, the doting old
grandfather - all cast aside, and probably forever, by the
momentary folly of a boy; then of his connection with the
ship-mutiny - unquestionably one of the most horrible
positions in which it is ever the fate of man to stand; the death
of his friend and his friend's father; the shipwreck, and the
long, lonely days of watching, in hunger and thirst, for a sail;
the final loss of all companions save a gorilla-like half-breed,
whose animal instinct of love and fidelity fell about the poor
boy like a protecting garment. Then comes this bright spot in
his life away in Hili-liland, like a momentary rift in the clouds
of a stormy day. For Pym the sun shone with a heavenly
effulgence, whilst the obstructions of a dire destiny were for a
time removed; but when again the clouds closed between him
and the brightness of existence, they closed forevermore. Yet
this mere boy, into whose life hardship and danger had
introduced more than the experience of most old men,
enjoyed, too, what many very aged men never have possessed -
what Alexander the Great never possessed - that of which
wealth or other source of power seems actually to deprive
many men. He enjoyed what was worth more than all that
ambition backed by wealth and power can give - that is, the
faithful love of a beautiful woman, loved truly in return. This
boy was loved by one who was capable with her witching
loveliness of satisfying every desire, enthralling the
imagination, rousing in the heart that passion which inspires

the mind to regions where it throbs in harmony with the Divine, and touches - as might some dying desert-waif with his parched lips a cooling fountain - the very source of love itself. But the most of human love - how debased and debasing, how vile! God, for purposes of His own, links for mankind the Aphroditic passion to the love Divine. The two are separable, and man assuredly separates them. True love may be witnessed as low in the scale of life, and as high, as consciousness is found. We find it in the heart of the faithful animal that dies on a loved master's grave, howling in anguish its life away. And we find it in the purity of woman's heart, where it rests ready for the contact that is to ignite it into illumination forever. Woman herself is divine. Man has placed her everywhere, sometimes behind the barred doors of a harem, sometimes on the throne of empire; but he has not blotted out the divine.

"With Pym it may not have been a love that would have carried him safely into and through a beatific old age - or it may have been; we choose to think that it was a growth that would have bloomed perennially. It was, I think, such a love as every man of imagination feels to be a mountain of wealth beside which all else is dwarfed to utter nothingness - a concretion from the endless and eternal ocean of love - a glimpse into that paradise where exists the Almighty, who is Love.

"I should judge from what Peters knows well enough, but which I gleaned by patient toil from that wicked though unsophisticated old segment of intelligence, that these two young persons had a most delightful, though extremely peculiar, wedding journey. The months had flown, until it was again December - the antarctic midsummer month, in which, and the greater part of January, there is no night.

"At this, the delightful season of the antarctic year, a beautiful yacht-like vessel was equipped; and with Peters as captain, and four men under his orders; Lilama, and a lady friend, with two maids; and Pym, accompanied by his now close friend, Diregus, the journey began.

"To Peters' mind, the most remarkable part of this pleasure excursion, was the extreme differences in climatic conditions which the party experienced within the range of a single day's, or even a single hour's travel. In December and January, Hili-li was so warm as scarcely to be habitable - certainly not comfortably habitable for natives of the central temperate zone of North America; yet at this same period of time, there was a small island on the meridian of Hili-li, and only thirty miles from the large surface-crater, on which the temperature was about 65 deg. F. There was, just across 'The Mountain' - as the Hili-lites frequently spoke of the rings of mountain-ranges surrounding the central crater - an island of somewhat greater area, upon which ice was at all times to be found at a few feet above sea-level, and which, during eight months of the year, was so cold that no animal life could have existed upon it. Then, at variable distances from the crater, and in different directions, islands were to be found of almost any desired temperature. The wealthier Hili-lites owned summer residences on these out-lying islands, situated at sailing distances varying from an hour to six hours' travel from Hili-li.

"The wedding-party, owing to the social position or the personal qualities of its members - which included official rank, hereditary prestige, beauty, mental culture, and preternatural prowess - was everywhere warmly welcomed. It was expected, received with open arms, and every source of entertainment was exhausted to make its visit at each island enjoyable.

"The party visited the island owned by Lilama, where they found the temperature quite cold, but the island comfortably habitable. It was at about the same distance from the crater as was Hili-li; and was so situated as to be of nearly one temperature all the year round. They found at work there a body of men, numbering not more than fifteen or twenty. It seems that upon making a trial of the various islands as a home for the descendants of the animals brought south by the original settlers, it was found that upon this island conditions were the best for raising sheep for their wool; and from the wool raised, Lilama's income was much greater than from the precious stones found there later, though precious stones were found on no other island in Hili-liland. Peters knows next to nothing, either theoretically or practically, of geology; but he says this island looked very different from the others in that region, and that its mountainous central portion appeared altogether different from any other of the mountains in Hili-liland. Asked to say if he had ever seen a mountain-range which Lilama's mountain resembled, he replied, but could not say why he so thought, that it reminded him of various parts of the Appalachian range.

"In strolling about the island, the party entered a small warehouse in which the precious stones were kept. Peters says that the gems which he there saw were of all sizes up to a large hen-egg, and of all colors except green. He particularly remembers being given several beautiful specimens, including blue, red, yellow, violet, gray, and white stones, all transparent; a black stone, and a brown-gray opaque stone. These were, of course, the sapphire, ruby, topaz, amethyst, and other varieties of corundum, the islands evidently containing no emeralds or diamonds. Lilama selected from a tray a stone the color of pigeon-blood, and about the size of an English walnut, which she handed to Pym as she might have handed him a beautiful rose. In Europe or America this stone would have purchased a fair-sized town.

"Peters described a strange natural phenomenon that exists on an island not more than half a mile in length, which the party visited after leaving Lilama's island. Near the centre of this last-mentioned island, says Peters, is a volcanic mountain about four thousand feet in height, with an extinct crater reaching down through the centre of the mountain to within a hundred feet of the sea-level, and, at its lower part, communicating with the outer surface by a tunnel some ten feet in diameter. Upon entering, by means of the tunnel, this sunken crater, a gallery was found, ascending spirally by at least twenty turns to the extreme peak of the mountain. The diameter of the crater was about one hundred feet at the bottom, about two hundred feet at the top - the diameter widening at each complete circuit of the gallery by from eight to twelve feet, the breadth of the gallery varying from four feet to six. Looking from below at the opening above, the spot of sky, says Peters, looked like the full moon. The length of the gallery, as its gradient is about forty-five degrees, must be about a mile and a half. Out of the gallery, at several points in the ascent, passes a small side-tunnel, communicating with the exterior.

"On still another island, about a hundred miles from Hili-li, but on about the same meridian - that is to say, in the same warm air-current, though the heat of the current was there much diminished by dilution - the party visited certain ruins which had always greatly puzzled the Hili-lites. The island was quite large, and was covered with agricultural farms, from which a single crop was taken each year. The ruins were quite uninjured by time; and one small stone structure was so complete as to be scarcely more dilapidated in appearance than would be any other old and neglected stone building in Hili-li. The stone of which the various structures were composed had never in all the centuries of their residence there been found by the Hili-lites elsewhere than in these buildings; the supposition being that it came from the great surrounding continent. But, after all, the real peculiarity of these buildings was in their architecture. The difficulty of obtaining from Peters any architectural facts, you will never appreciate unless you attempt, as I have done, to procure such information. He declares that in these buildings were neither columns nor arches; and he also declares that the absence of arches and columns he knows, not only from his own observation, but because that fact was alluded to in his presence by the Hili-lite members of the party; yet he is equally certain that in one of the larger of the ruins the roof was intact. How a roof could be supported without reasonable vertical resistance, and without arch resistance, I am unable to say; and it is wholly improbable that the walls in a building of its dimensions could, without an arch, support a roof. The Hellenes, you recall, were very artful in hiding from observation the arch, though they frequently employed it. I admit that I must have greatly bored old man

Peters over this subject of architecture; and as I myself know next to nothing of the subject, technically, and he knows absolutely nothing of it, technically or otherwise, and as he took no interest in the ruins even when they were before his eyes, you will understand that my information concerning these ruins is not very clear. It was also utterly impossible for me to gain from the old man data upon which to base an opinion as to the style of architecture of these structures. The buildings generally were very large, very beautiful, and constructed in a style entirely distinct from any known ancient style - that is, for instance, they were not Hellenic, or Egyptian, or Assyrian, or Roman. This much the Hili-lites knew and said. Then, further, there were inscriptions in characters unknown to the world at the time of the barbarian overflow into the Roman Empire, and also unknown to Pym. In one of the ruins was a large window made of blue and yellow transparent corundum, in which appeared an inscription made by a setting of rubies.

"What a strange world, in which entire races come and go, some of them leaving a ruin or two, and perhaps an odd indecipherable inscription here and there! The world was fortunate indeed to grasp, from the obliterated and forgotten past, Hebraism and Hellenism - the moral and the beautiful; from which man's craving for goodness has resulted in Christianity; and from which his impulses of sweetness and brightness and loveliness have developed the Renascence! Between goodness and beauty, why should there ever be conflict? Pure goodness is pure love, and love is almost synonymous with beauty. - But, pardon the digression.

"The tour of the islands comprising Hili-liland continued through December and January. I could tell you much of the social gayeties in many a bright country-home during these two months; but in these Peters was not much interested, and I could not get from him many of the particulars. Thus far I have striven to keep all facts unpolluted by any possible alloy of my own imagination - let me continue to be, in word and in spirit, true to the facts. Were I to attempt a description of these island festivities in faraway Hili-liland, perhaps, inadvertently - the facts being meagre - I might say something bordering on untruth; and, rather than untruth - a thousand times rather - silence.

"I will close for this evening by saying that the wedding-party arrived at the island of Hili-li about February 1st - the year being 1829. Some time before starting on the tour, Lilama had begun the construction of a new home; and by the time of her return it was completed. Her new residence was not large, but it was elegant. Here the happy couple dwelt, Peters having an apartment to himself which was enough to set a sailor wild with joy. Peters says that he grew to like very much what he calls 'volcano tobacco;' that it was 'good and strong' - to his taste all the better for that. The only mistake that Lilama's architect made in his plan for her new home was in not having Peters' apartment either on the roof, or else next door. Peters now smokes American tobacco; and even now - but let the past go; I did not sit on the edge of the old sailor's bed for thirty hours for nothing. Tomorrow evening I shall tell you of the great catastrophe which occurred on the island of Hili-li during the visit of Pym and Peters."

Here Bainbridge closed his recital for the evening. I believe that he would have remained for at least a few minutes longer; but as he was about to reply to a question of mine, Castleton rushed into the room, and Bainbridge departed.

Castleton, who was overflowing with joyous excitement, informed me that the dreaded yellow fever of the South was on its way North; and that if I would delay my return to England for a week or ten days I could see it. His remark did not much alarm me. Then I proceeded to tell him in outline what had become of Ahpilus, of the marriage of Lilama and Pym, and of the wedding-tour of the islands. As I closed, he said:

"Young man, you will soon be returning to England, that lordly nation to whose hind-quarters the sun is kinder than to its head-quarters. When you get home tell your countrymen of the discoveries you have here made. Tell them of the wonders of Hili-li - but be careful. This fellow Bainbridge is a romantic youth, and he is liable to lead you astray in some important respects. Tell your noble countrymen of the central crater - that, no doubt, Peters saw; as to the Hili-lites being descendants of the pure stock of ancient Rome, that, too, I believe. But do not repeat this foolish theory about love which he introduces into Peters' narrative. The wise, practical, and puissant residents of that Corinthian Capital of Brains - I refer to London - will know better. Oh, yes; women are true! - very true! Better than wealth - pshaw! better than empire - pooh! That nonsense will pass at twenty-five; at forty a man has some brains. The 'constancy' of women - that gets me! Why, sir, I once loved three women at the same time, and not one of the three was true to me - yet Bainbridge talks of a woman's constancy, single-heartedness, and such chimerical stuff - the kind of stuff, that, with youth, takes the place of the recently discarded nursery fiction. I think of the hundreds of women that I have loved, beginning in my early boyhood, passing through my adolescence to the acme of my powers, and even now as I stand on the verge of my desuetude! Surely some one of these many women would have been constant, if women have any constancy in their make-up. Show me a woman howling out her life on *my* grave, and then I'll believe Bainbridge. But I know all about Bainbridge. I know where he goes the evenings that he doesn't come here. Never mind - I'm silent as the grave. I don't need to tell a man of your superlative acumen what Bainbridge's talk implies. He mustn't talk to me though about woman's constancy and single-heartedness till he's ten years older; let him tell that stuff to Peters and the other mariners."

After some further talk, Castleton remarked:

"It seems, then, according to Bainbridge, that we moderns owe about all we have to the Jew and the Dago! Now, men less intelligent than you and I, after looking at the average Jew and Dago as seen to-day in the United States, would doubt this assertion. I cannot dispute it, however; for through the ancient

Jew certainly came Christianity, and through the ancients in Greece and Italy our art."

He paused for a moment, and then continued:

"A delightfully euphonious set of names those Hili-lites possess. The name *Hi_li-_li* is not bad itself: *Hili-li*, *Hili-lite*, *Hili-li*land - pretty good. *Li*-la-ma, Ah-*pe*-lus, Di-*re*-gus, Me-*do*-sus, Ma-*su*-se-*li*-la - all pretty fair. I have no doubt that Bainbridge would spell them so as to produce a Latin appearance. And this reminds me of a certain name not Latin."

I saw that the doctor was about to recount a "personal experience." He continued:

"One day a stranger came to our town - a plain, clean-looking, blue-eyed sort of scientific fellow from somewhere so far out in the suburbs of Europe that the name of his country or province has wholly slipped my memory - a mighty rare thing, by the by, and it always galls me when I forget anything. This chap came here to look at coal, or to hammer rocks, or to look for curiosities. Well, he ran up against me. Don't ask me his name - I believe he spelled it S-c-h-w-o-j-k-h-h-j-z-y-t-y-h-o B-j-h-z-o-w-h-j-u-g-h-s-c-h-k-j. One day he asked me to introduce him to a certain Bellevue capitalist. The fellow had pleased me, and I agreed to do the introducing - partly, I admit, to see whether a man that gutteralled his words out of his stomach could swindle one of our own sharpers that talked through his nose. But now came the rub: how was I to introduce a man when I couldn't utter his name? I used to practice at pronouncing that name as I rode around in my buggy, but it was no go. At last the day came when I was to introduce the fellow with a surplus of knowledge, to the fellow with a surplus of cash. That morning I awoke with the worst sorethroat of my life. I felt as if I had two boiled potatoes in my throat. The passage from my nose to my windpipe was closed for repairs, and that from my mouth to my throat was seven-eighths closed. Pretty soon, just from recent habit, I began to practise on the scientific chap's name. Great Scott! I could pronounce it better than its owner could. There were certain grunts and sneezes in the name - particularly one syllable between a grunt and a sneeze - that I suppose no Anglo-Saxon had ever before or has ever since uttered correctly; but they were nothing to me, so long as my sorethroat lasted."

Then Castleton rushed from the room; calling back from the head of the stairs, and in tones intentionally audible to every man and woman on that floor of the hotel:

"It's coming, sir, depend upon it - the genuine yellow fever - evaded the New Orleans quarantine three weeks ago - three cases at Shreveport and two at Memphis reported - talk, too, of a case in St. Louis. Heavens! But I hope a beneficent Creator will not allow some other doctor to get the first case, when, happily, it shall have reached Bellevue."

The last sentence was uttered *sotto voce*, as he descended the stairs.

THE EIGHTEENTH CHAPTER

"It appears," continued Bainbridge, on the following evening, "that Hili-li was subject to the recurrence about once in forty-seven years of a strange thermic phenomenon, the mean duration of which was about fifty hours. This change had occurred twenty-one times in the preceding thousand years; its duration had once been as brief as thirty hours, and at another time had lasted one hundred and twenty hours. The interval between two of its visitations had once been somewhat less than eight years; whilst at the period of Pym and Peters' presence in Hili-li, it had not occurred for eighty-six years and some months. For some reason that could not be conjectured, at these times the wind-currents, generally varying but slightly in force and duration, changed, the wind coming from a point of the compass almost diametrically opposite to its usual direction, and increasing in velocity and force to that of a tempest or blizzard. The result was, that in a very few hours the temperature of Hili-li fell to about zero Fahrenheit, if in December or January; to 60 deg. or 70 deg. Fahrenheit below freezing, if in July or August. During the first few hours of the change, owing to the extremely moist state of the atmosphere for many miles in all directions from the crater of Hili-li, there occurred a heavy snowfall - which, however, diminished as the temperature fell, until at somewhat above the zero point it ceased.

"The government of Hili-li, by laws and by the encouragement of custom, did much to prevent damage from these storms - which, as I have intimated, were a combination of hurricane and snow-storm, with a very sudden and rapid fall of temperature; and when the interval between two of them was not greater than twenty years, the provisions made by the state were ample to prevent loss of life. By the law of the land, residence houses had to be built in such a manner that at least one room in each house could be warmed by a fire. Fire for purposes of warmth was never in Hili-li required, except during these storms; and all cooking was done on a peculiar stove made chiefly of gold, the fuel of which was either fish oil, or another oil termed by the boatmen who sold it 'continent oil' - or, rather, by a name corresponding in the Hili-li language to those words in the English. The law further provided that on the premises of each home wood should be kept, ready for use, in chests of a size convenient for two persons to carry into the room in which it was to be burned. By this means, the worst that could happen to a family was that its members might suddenly at any time be confined to a single room, comfortably warmed, for from thirty to a hundred hours, or thereabouts. Even if there should be very little food in any one home, or if the wood supply should be neglected, the next door neighbor could be relied upon for succor.

"Ninety-four years prior to the summer that now concerns us, a cold spell had occurred after an interval of eighty-one years, which lasted a hundred and ten hours, and during which one-third of the inhabitants of Hili-li, between hunger and cold, lost their lives. Not more than one hundred persons remembered the last preceding storm, and they must have been very young children when it occurred; and even they felt no alarm on the subject, as the storm preceding it had happened about sixteen years earlier, and, though a light one, was sufficient to alarm both the rulers and the masses, and resulted in a state of preparedness for the next storm. But now, the middle-aged men knew of these cold spells only as matters of history, to which they gave little practical attention; and from the lips of their grandparents, who, as I have said, had never personally known one of them to cause serious distress or loss of life.

"On the morning of February 17, 1829, there was not on the Island of Hili-li a single residence which had the wood-supply contemplated by the forgotten statute relating to that subject; there were few homes that had in store food sufficient for more than forty-eight hours use; and, though most families were in possession of some oil, their cook-stoves were not constructed for heating, and were connected with flues in outbuildings; and, further, there was not enough oil on the island to have warmed the city at such a time for twenty-four hours.

"It must also be remembered that the Hili-lites were accustomed to a temperature, all the year through, year in and year out, of 90 deg. to 108 deg. Fahrenheit scale; and that for a resident of England, or of the United States above the latitude of Washington City, a temperature of ten degrees below zero would be quite as well borne as would a temperature of thirty degrees above zero by these islanders. There was little physical and mental inurement to cold, and the lightest of clothing was worn. A resident of Hili-li, when business compelled him to visit an island on which the temperature was cold enough to freeze water, prepared himself personally for the journey as would a Swede or Norwegian for a journey of exploration to the North Pole.

"In the night between February 16th and 17th, Peters, who was in the habit in Hili-li of sleeping *in puris naturalibus*, awoke in a shiver. He arose, and closing his window-sash began to look around his room for bed-covering; but he found only a sheet, and a very fine wool bedspread, which he drew over him as he once more assumed a recumbent position. He again fell asleep; but in an hour awoke, shivering harder than before. He then dressed, and lighting his pipe, walked up and down the floor. Then he looked from the window, and saw that a fine snow was falling, the separately almost invisible flakes whirling in sharp spirals as they fell. The sailor instinct - the aptitude of the navigator - instantly told him what this thermic change meant for Hili-li. Others in the house were now moving about, and Peters sought them out. Pym did not seem at once to realize the danger; and Lilama said she had heard of these storms, but did not think that they lasted long. All except Peters were wrapped in shawl-like garments, and some of the servants had about their forms light rugs which they had taken from the floors. Soon, however, all except Pym and Peters were shivering; and every article of covering obtainable was in use. Lilama told a maid to bring out her dresses and wrappers, which she divided among the servants, each donning several garments. Peters, stoical, but always on the alert, called Pym aside, and explained to him that this change meant nothing less than the devastation of Hili-li - that the temperature was steadily falling, the wind increasing, and that the storm was only beginning. Pym could not but perceive that the cold was due to a pronounced alteration in the direction of wind-currents; and that under the circumstances the cold would of necessity increase to the point of normal antarctic temperature - no doubt below zero - unless the wind should before then change. Quickly his mind grasped the circumstances in which they were placed. They were on an island, situated in water navigable at all seasons and hours, with the chief food-supply on near-by islands, and each day brought to Hili-li for that day's consumption; they were in a city practically without fuel; the inhabitants were accustomed to heat, and wholly unused to cold; the houses were built without protection against cold, because, except occasionally for a few hours at a time, there were no climatic conditions demanding such a construction. Further, the climate being very warm, there was not - except in the possession of a hundred men whose business took them on visits to islands lying outside of the crater-warmed air-currents - a heavy wrap of any kind, such as overcoat, cloak, or shawl, in the entire city. Carpets were not known in Hili-li, so it would be impossible for the hard-pressed people to retire to bed, where, covering the body with a few sheets and some clothing, they might add the carpets, and, in hunger but in safety, remain protected against those freezing blasts till the wind should change. Pym comprehended the terrible position in which Lilama and the other Hili-lites stood; the extremity of desolation which must soon prevail standing out before him like a vivid picture, and for a moment overawing even his brave, true soul. He did not doubt that Peters and himself could withstand the cold, though they might not be able to obtain more than a flimsy shelter from the biting antarctic winds. He scarcely thought of himself - he thought only of Lilama, and, in a measure, of the other residents of the beautiful, stricken city. Exposure to danger had made Pym in times of trouble a rapid thinker, and the thoughts which I have mentioned passed through his mind in less than a minute of time. Then he turned to Lilama, and asked if there was beneath the house a cellar. Fortunately there was - the house was one of the few in Hili-li beneath a portion of which a cellar was constructed as a depository, and as a protection against heat for certain articles of food, most of the residents not caring to construct cellars; articles of food easily destructible by heat being twice daily brought to the city and distributed to the houses, and ice costing only the expense of shipping it by water some six or eight hours' sailing distance.

"Pym and Peters moved about the house, making certain arrangements so rapidly as to startle the languid Hili-lites. In ten or fifteen minutes they had removed to the cellar all the necessary furniture of a comfortable room, including a bedstead for Lilama, and another for her two maids. Three lamps were taken to the cellar, lighted, and oil sufficient for a week's consumption placed conveniently near. The house contained enough food to sustain Lilama, and the women servants, for from six to eight days. Within twenty minutes of the time Peters had suggested to Pym the danger of freezing to be apprehended, Lilama and her maids were safely placed in the cellar, and were making merry over their strange surroundings and attire. Then Pym and Peters hastened from the house, to see what could be done for others.

"And now was witnessed the influence on man, of heredity and environment, and the insurmountable difficulties in the way, even under the most pressing need, of overcoming such influence. The Hili-lites in more than a thousand years had fought only one battle, and that five hundred years before; nor had they found necessary any struggle for food, or against rigorous climate. They were a brainy people, and were almost superhumanly perceptive in every sense organ and in every nerve. But they were wanting in that quality possessed by most European peoples and by Americans, which takes practical cognizance of the fact that prompt action and fearlessness is the true protection against danger. In the face of this great calamity among the Hili-lites, even the leading men seemed paralyzed. Not that they displayed a particle of fear - it was simply not in them to move rapidly, and to face joyfully great dangers. With them, when mental processes failed to subdue, there was not much left. They could have conquered a modern warship, provided they could have come in contact with its officers, by controlling in some strange way the minds of those men; but against a storm, or the course of inanimate nature in any other direction, they were as powerless as any other people, and their sense of powerlessness was paralyzing to them. On the other hand, Pym and Peters had sprung from races that had in the past thousand years gone through hundreds of struggles, amid every kind of danger, for existence; and Peters, on the mother's side, she being an American Indian, belonged to a race which had gone through what was infinitely worse than a barbarian invasion - namely, a 'civilized' and 'enlightened' invasion. These two men seemed to court danger - to revel in it; but in reality they pursued the course which exposed them to the least risk of injury consistent with the performance of their full duty. The question was one of method in procedure to save the greatest number of lives; and they hastened first to the residence of Lilama's uncle and cousin - to the home of the Duke and Diregus."

Charles Romyn Dake

THE NINETEENTH CHAPTER

Arriving there, they found the Duke and Diregus quite actively engaged - for Hili-lites; still, very much valuable time was being wasted. Already the snow had ceased to fall, and the temperature, Peters thinks, must have reached ten degrees below freezing, and was rapidly falling. In the ducal palace there were, in two or three rooms, hearths, and flue-openings for carrying off smoke; but as there was no wood ready for burning, and as there seemed to be no dry wood in sight, the Duke and his son were at the end of their resources as soon as they had gathered together into a safe place food sufficient to last for a week or ten days. Fortunately the palace was unusually well stocked with edibles.

When Pym and Peters arrived, their cool manner and prompt action exhaling confidence with every look and movement, the Duke and Diregus were soon enlivened, as in fact were all others who came in contact with these two active and intrepid strangers.

Pym glanced about him, compassing at a look all possible resources. Then he issued his orders, himself working with the others, and, so to speak, 'setting the pace.' In ten minutes a large outbuilding - similar to our summer-houses, or Anglo-Saxon kiosks - was razed to the ground, broken in pieces, and placed in the rooms, in which fires were soon glowing and crackling. In twenty minutes, those whom Pym and Peters had found half-frozen and wholly discouraged, were cheerful, comfortable, and out of danger.

The two men hastened forth through the city, giving assistance and advice, and infusing confidence. The smaller residences, as well as many of those of medium size, were constructed of wood. Pym went rapidly through the city, ordering that one house in each square be demolished, and the wood divided - but haste! haste! The temperature was rapidly declining to a point at which a Hili-lite, even when actively at work, could not exist.

Pym and Peters might, unaided, have reached one-tenth of the people of Hili-li, and have shown them the way to safety. As many more, possibly, might have found other means of saving themselves. It seems improbable that more than one-fourth of the people of Hili-li would have survived this terrible storm, had Pym and Peters not been reinforced.

"Let no man, in his finite weakness, ever question the methods of Infinite Wisdom, which is Infinite Goodness. At the very time when every moment gained by Pym and Peters meant the saving of a hundred more lives - at the very moment when two additional men, hardy and inured to danger, would have doubled the life-saving force, four hundred of the 'Exiles of Olympus' arrived in the city. They had left behind them warmth and safety, and sailing across thirty miles of tempestuous sea, had come, headed by Medosus, to try to save their fellow-countrymen. These four hundred men, young and vigorous, comprised the real enterprise and daring of Hili-li. They had been promised their liberty, and their visits, individually, to Hili-li had recently been not only allowed but even encouraged by those in authority; but the final act permitting them to return had been, by the formalities of state, delayed.

"Pym, Peters, and Medosus consulted for a moment, and then the exiles divided into a hundred parties of four each, and systematically scattered through the city, doing the work of giants. Finally the exiles established a hundred stations, selecting for the purpose large rooms, in which they built hearths of lava-blocks taken from the streets, in most of the houses the hearths being placed in the centre of an upper room, and an opening directly above cut through the roof. At each of these stations one exile at a time took charge of the fire, whilst the other three of the party in charge scoured the neighborhood for persons that might in the first desultory search have been overlooked. Then, when all seemed provided for, the exiles, protecting their bodies with such additional clothing as those now cared for could spare, went forth in search of food, to the deserted houses, and to such depots of supply as the city possessed.

"The work of rescue being thoroughly inaugurated, Pym had a moment in which his mind might roam from the work immediately in hand; and he thought of the aged mystic, Masusaelili. The old man resided in a spot so retired that the various rescue parties might easily have overlooked him; and the temperature was now probably fifty degrees below freezing. Fortunately, at the instant he thought of the old philosopher, he and Peters were near the city limits, and within a third of a mile of Masusaelili's home; and starting off at a brisk run, the two were five minutes later in the old man's house, standing outside his laboratory door. As the two had hurried along, Peters would continue to murmur against the project: 'What's the use,' he would growl; 'we'll only find the old fellow roasting himself in front of a magic fire of burning snow or ice. *He's* all right, and we'd better be saving human people.'

"As several raps, increasing from the gentlest to the most vigorous, elicited no response, Pym opened the laboratory door, and with Peters entered. But the old man was nowhere to be seen. Pym hastily returned to the hallway, and discovering a stair leading to a small cellar, he descended. The cellar was filled with *debris*, two small window casements opening to the exterior air were broken and decayed to the last degree of dilapidation, and the icy wind whistled through the rubbish of the doleful spot. He ran back to the laboratory, where Peters was hunting about, hoping to find Masusaelili alive, yet fearing to find his emaciated form lying lifeless amid the mass of chemical and mechanical appliances which littered the room. Several of the large vase-like objects before alluded to stood here and there; and as the smaller of them might have hidden the body of a large-sized man, the searchers even glanced into them. Each vase sat apart upon the floor, flaring upward like a giant lily to a height of four or five feet; and from each of them projected, within an inch of the floor, a faucet of rude construction, through which passed a very primitive spigot. One of these enormous vases, large enough to have secreted two small men, stood inverted; and Pym, with no particular object in view, but simply because he could not think of anything else to do, gave the vase a push, in such a way as to raise for an inch or two from the floor its large rim, flaring out to a diameter of probably four feet.

"'Put that down,' came a hollow and stridulous voice, so unexpected and startling to Pym that he withdrew his hand, allowing the vase to drop back to the floor with a resounding thud.

"'If thou hast aught of importance to impart, 'continued the voice - that of Masusaelili - still stridulous, but now having also the quality possessed by a voice heard through a speaking-tube, 'put thy mouth near to the spigot-hole, and disclose thine errand.'

"Pym placed his lips within an inch of the open faucet, which was only an inch or two lower than his mouth as he stood beside the vase, and from the opening of which came a fog-like vapor, similar in appearance to that exhaled from the mouth and nostrils on a very cold day, and said:

"'We came, sir, to offer our help - to procure for you wood, and, if possible, food; or, if you should so prefer, to remove you in safety to comfortable quarters.'

"For a moment there was silence, during which the fog-like vapor continued to come from the spigot-hole of the inverted vase. Then the voice of the aged mystic was again heard in reply:

"'Youth - and thine ape-like companion - go hence. Through three and fifty of these storms have I safely passed. Beneath this vase have I two lamps, alight; oil wherewith to supply with fuel these two lamps for a space of eight days, which hitherto has been the longest duration of any of these periodical storms; food and water have I sufficient for my body's wants for a week. And, too, have I mental aliment; for have I here a manuscript written by the youthful sage, AEgyptus, who sent it to me by the hand of Azza, long before the legend of Romulus started from its mythic source to float adown the stream of time: a manuscript which it delighteth my soul once in each century to peruse. Fear not for one who knows no fear. Go hence, and quickly go - go with humiliation in thy heart; for thou hast not yet begun to live, and yet thou presumest to think in danger one who helped to plan and to construct what thou callest the ancient city of Babylon. Youth, when thou didst disturb me, I was reading from my friend, who writes from a village called Sakkarah, of how a foolish Pharaoh thinks to perpetuate his memory by building a mighty pyramidal structure of stone, which my friend terms a device planned by himself to divert the fancy of his ruler, and incidentally to astonish those European barbarians who may happen that way; and, among other matters, this Azza asks for my opinion concerning the outer surface of his pyramid; to which request for advice I remember that I replied, saying that the walls should be constructed so as to ascend in step-like angles. Ha, ha, ha!' came from the spigot-hole a hollow, cracked attempt at derisive laughter - 'Ye say - ha, ha! - ye say this Pharaoh was of the *first* dynasty! - ha, ha! - the first! Go hence, vain child.'

"'But, sir,' insisted Pym, after a pause, 'have you provided for ventilating your - your small apartment?'

"'In the floor beneath me is a knot-hole, which doth open to the outer air; and upon the opening is a flat stone, which, little by little, more or less, I remove and replace in accordance with certain laws, allowing just the proper amount of atmospheric air to enter from below. This oil maketh very little smoke, yet seest thou not some smoke emerge from the open faucet?

Feel'st thou not with thine hand the heat escape? Again I say, go hence, vain youth.'

"Pym stood for a moment, meditating; and then something - perhaps something connected with the words several months before whispered into his ear by Masusaelili - impelled him to say:

"'Good sir, we meant you no harm. Tell me, Allwise One, can you read the future?'

"Before a reply came, there was a pause so long that, says Peters, Pym was about to speak again. Then came the voice of this old man who had investigated and pondered for thousands of years that only inexhaustible study in the universe, the phenomenon of consciousness - the aged mystic no doubt being pleasantly warmed and mollified by the appellation 'Allwise One.'

"'None but God,' said Masusaelili, 'knows of a certainty the future. Truly wise men, and the lower animals, when they would penetrate the future, use not the crude instrument termed *reason*; but rather do they nestle close to the bosom of - what now call ye Him? Thine ancestors, the barbarians of Britannia, when I was with them, named Him God. Thus, and only thus, may the future become known to thee. Have faith, as the bird, the fish, the little ant, which, *feeling* God, act, and are not disappointed. Think ye that the lowest of God's creatures would not have heard His warning voice, or seen His beckoning arm, or felt His guiding hand when in the air lurked this present danger? Yet reason told not you! God shows to us the future, when we should know His edicts in advance, always - always, if only we will look and hearken. But this, good youth, God doth permit only to those who lean with full confidence upon Him, as do the lower animals. To the consciousness of man it is given, if but the right conditions be attained, truly to know what in the present happeneth anywhere in the universe. *Time* is a barrier to the voluntary acquisition of knowledge, but *distance* is not an impediment.

Charles Romyn Dake

My body is confined to this poor vase, but certainly not my mind - it roams in Europe, in Asia, or amid the stars - but wait a moment. Poor youth! The hand on the dial of thy destiny moves rapidly. Go! Go now, and go in haste; for one who loves thee, at this moment sorely needs thee. Farewell.'

"Pym scarcely heard the word 'farewell;' for he was crossing the threshold of the house as Masusaelili uttered it, and Peters was turning to follow. They ran as rapidly as the snow and the cutting wind would permit, and had covered the necessary three miles in about half an hour. The air was growing intensely cold. They met a party of three exiles, who were helping to scour the city for any food that might have been left in deserted homes. These men informed Pym that, in spite of the promptitude and haste of the rescue parties, more than a hundred persons had been frozen to death; and that frozen hands and feet by the thousand had been reported. The Hililites were so extremely susceptible to cold that, at a temperature of 20 deg. Fahrenheit, if they were not well protected by clothing, they soon became drowsy, then slept, and, if not found and resuscitated within a very short time, died. One case was reported in which a woman, only six hundred feet from one of the rescue stations, was frozen to death in somewhat less than an hour, though she must have been thoroughly chilled when last seen in an apparently natural condition. During the day a party of three exiles, whilst on one of their rounds, had visited the house of this poor woman, and had carried her three children to the nearest station; and the woman herself, who was at the time hurrying about the room gathering together a few articles, it was supposed had followed close behind them. In this way she was overlooked, until, in the somewhat crowded room to which the children were taken, the youngest child, a little girl of four years, broke into tears and began to cry out for her mother. Then two men hastened back, and found the woman unconscious and apparently dead. The usual methods of resuscitation were inaugurated, and long continued, but the woman could not be revived.

"Peters says that he has during his life-time seen a number of persons who were frozen, several of them fatally; of which a part were in the Eastern States, others in the far north; and that these Hili-lites froze to death very differently from those in the northern part of the north temperate zone. He mentions the case of a Canadian who was exposed to extreme cold during a whole night. When found, the poor fellow was not only unconscious, but apparently dead. The arms and legs were frozen through and through, and the entire body was rigid. He was resuscitated, but afterwards lost his hands and feet. In Hili-li persons lost their lives from exposure to cold whose bodies were very little - a few of them not at all - frozen. The explanation of this difference is to be found in the fact that an animal dies when bodily temperature in the interior of the body reaches a certain degree of reduction, which point of reduction in the Hili-lites is much less than in persons habituated to life in a colder climate. In persons accustomed to a climate as warm as that of Hili-li, the heat-producing functions are feeble, and the heat-expelling functions are very active; but this does not fully explain why, in Peters' words, 'the people there froze to death without freezing.' Any person dying as a result of exposure to cold, dies long before any of the vital organs are frozen; and the Hili-lites no doubt ceased to live with a reduction of bodily temperature which would not have seriously inconvenienced a resident of Scotland or Canada. In the storm of which we speak, the people were nervously depressed as a result of fright. However, from all I can gather, the temperature was at times certainly as low as 40 deg. Fahrenheit below freezing, at which degree almost any thinly clad person might freeze to death.

"But the hour is late, and, though I had expected to close Peters' story this evening, such a conclusion is, owing to my prolixity, scarcely practicable. If you still expect to start for home in three days, I shall certainly in one more evening complete the telling of Peters' experiences in Hili-li. The day after tomorrow I shall be engaged during the entire evening, and if we delay our next meeting till the following evening - your last in Bellevue - it is possible that something may happen to prevent our meeting; so, if you are willing, my next and last visit to you here shall be tomorrow evening."

I expressed my satisfaction with the arrangement, and he took his leave.

The following morning, I gave to Arthur, in my own way, an account of the storm in Hili-li, meanwhile leisurely dressing - a performance which, except under pressure, I have never in the morning been able unaided to accomplish in less than an hour. I had completed my toilet, but not my story, when in rushed Castleton.

After a little general conversation, I seemed naturally to return to the Peters story; and now, in a five-minute talk, I so closed it to the point reached by Bainbridge as to satisfy Arthur, and not weary the restless doctor. As I ended, Castleton said:

"I didn't get in to see you yesterday. The last time I was in we were talking of names; and to tell you the truth, it was a matter of names that held me back yesterday at the very time I was going to come up. You see, I have an old friend here in town, -; you've no doubt heard of him - ex-member of Congress, and as good as appointed Minister to Venezuela right now. A scholar of the deepest erudition; a speaker and writer of great force and nicety, and of exquisite literary taste. Yesterday we met, and during our talk he told me that his book, the result of many years of thought, was completed. Now, for my part, I never believed that a rose would smell as sweet as it does if we called it a turnip. If Poe had, instead of 'Narrative of A. Gordon Pym,' named his story, 'Adventures of Dirk Peters, the Half-Breed,' he would have sold twice as many books. My friend is about to publish his book. 'Its name?' I asked him. 'There can be little choice of names for a translation of Montesquieu's "Grandeur and Decadence of the Romans," with notes by myself,' he replied. 'There can't?' said I; 'well, my friend, let me tell you there can. Now compare this name: "Montesquieu's Considerations on the Causes of the Grandeur and Decadence of the Romans, with illustrative notes," etc., with a name like this: "The Roman Aristocrats Ripped, Rooted, and Routed"; or, "How the Roman Plutocrats were Peppered and Pounded." Heavens and Earth! what do the masses know about decadence? Why not name his book (and so I said to him), "How the Rich Romans Rotted"? Half the people would think from such a title that the Romans were enemies of the United States, and that Montesquieu and my friend were after them hot and fast; and then the story would go out that the French were helping us again. "General Montesquieu" would be heard on all sides, associated with endless repetitions of Lafayette memories. Lord, Lord! I sometimes think a man is better under-educated than over-educated."

Then after a pause he continued:

"Pretty good, that talk of Masusaelili's through the faucet - pretty good, pretty good! But, pshaw! for me there's nothing new on earth. Why, sir, I've always drawn my best philosophy out of a spigot-hole. The very sight of a spigot inspires me, and drives away my troubles. But, man alive! We must keep this thing secret. The fellow with an exhaustless stock of *elixir vitae* isn't half worked out in fiction yet - and besides, how can a person reread his 'Wandering Jew,' and his 'Last Days of Pompeii,' and his 'Zanoni,' with such an outlandish picture as a mystic under a lamp-warmed vase in mind? Why didn't Bainbridge take a not unusual historical license, and say that the aged philosopher was found warming himself before a crystal vase filled with magically glowing rubies?"

After we had laughed a little over this, he said:

"And I suppose Bainbridge tried - in fact I know by what you say that he did try - to air his knowledge on the subject of animal heat? No doubt talked for half an hour about the effects of cold on the animal economy? Oh, he's a rapid man! You heard, sir, how idiotically he talked that day, just before I cured old man Peters? If Bainbridge had had his way, Peters' story would have been a short one. I suppose his remedy for a frozen Hili-lite would be to send him to the North Pole! Now, sir, I instantly grasped the whole idea of the necessary effect of that cold wave on those Hili-lites, for I now have data in abundance for reading those people through and through. In a word, sir - and observe my sententious brevity - their thermo-genistic organization being adynamic, and their thermolysic functions being over-active owing to their thermic environ-ment, and the thermotaxic balance being habitually anomalous, the emergency was not successfully encountered; and this was more particularly the case because the nerve-centres of vital resistance to sudden and extreme thermal abstraction were atrophied."

This was the last remark, except a few words of farewell at the time of my departure for home, that I ever heard from Doctor Castleton. It was his habit, as he was about to leave the presence of an auditor or interlocutor, to fire off, so to speak, a set speech, or a piece of surprising information, and then hastily to retreat - a habit displaying considerable sagacity, and one engendered by street-corner discussion, in which a return fire - or perhaps a troublesome question - was often to be avoided if a dramatic climax was not to be sacrificed. On this occasion, as the last words left his lips he vanished through the doorway, and we were alone.

"Well," said Arthur, "am I allowed to speak?"

"You are," I replied.

"Then tell me," said he, "what it was he said? Why doesn't he, some day when he has time, dictate a dictionary? And isn't there any way to stop such talk by law? That man gets worse instead of better. He forgets everything except words. Says he, the other day, 'Well, Arthur, my boy, when are you coming in to pay your doctor bill?' Now mind, I paid him a'ready, and just think of my teeth! But I told him, nice and easy, how I paid him the two dollars. Then I told him about my teeth rattlin' whenever I go down the stairs, and asked him what to do for them. He just laughed and gave me a half-dollar, and said, 'Bone-set tea, my boy - drink bone-set tea, and plenty of it;' and so I do."

THE TWENTIETH CHAPTER

"Pym left the exiles," said Bainbridge, on the following evening, as, in accordance with his engagement, he continued the story of the great storm in Hili-li; "and hastened on toward his home. Arrived there, he went directly to the cellar, where he found the three large lamps alight, brilliantly illuminating and comfortably warming the apartment; but Lilama was missing, though he found there one of her maids. This girl told Pym that Lilama had, some four hours earlier, taken with her her maid Ixza, and hastened from the house. Questioned closely, she said that after Pym had gone, Lilama suddenly bethought her of a former servant, an old nurse, who for some years past had lived quite alone, and that Lilama had decided to have the poor old woman found, and cared for. It seems that when the young wife was herself in safety and had the mental leisure to think of others, the thought of her poor old servant and friend in danger grew more and more unbearable. She had waited almost an hour for Pym to return, and then, taking Ixza with her, had gone forth; but where the old nurse resided, only Lilama and Ixza knew. The maid knew only that Lilama had left the cellar with the intention of assisting, in some manner, the nurse of her babyhood.

"In ten minutes Pym and Peters, going in different directions, had aroused many of the exiles, who hastened in all directions, to search thoroughly the poorer quarters of the city, and to inquire of everyone whom they might encounter concerning the residence of the old nurse. The exiles had already visited, or sent others to visit, about every house in the city; but in a few instances - particularly where but one person lived in a house - the occupant had been advised, and had consented, to come to a central station and there remain till the storm abated or passed; and then, for some purpose delaying, had been overcome by the cold, and, as the system of search included only one visit to each house, had been left to die - the fact transpiring through an accidental second visit, or when the city was later scoured in search of food that might have been overlooked.

"An hour later, one of many messengers who were searching for Pym met him, and told him that Lilama was found. He hastened to the house in which they had found her - a small frame structure, the residence of her former nurse.

"At the entrance of this house stood Peters, waiting for his young friend; and as Pym felt the hand of the old sailor, put forth to stop him in his breathless haste, and as he looked into the hard, rugged face of his old friend, he knew that he must nerve himself for a shock. Alas! His surmise was only too correct. They entered the main room of the house together, Peters in the rear. Drawing aside from the entrance to the room a portiere - Peters had already visited the room - Pym passed in, Peters remaining on the outer side of the curtained doorway, that he might prevent others from following, or even from viewing the young friend who was now to receive one of the keenest stabs with which Destiny ever pierces the human heart.

"For a moment Pym would wholly have mistaken the scene before him, had Peters not said a word of warning as the portiere fell behind his young friend.

"On the lounge which stood against the farther wall as he entered, lay an elderly woman, apparently asleep; and covering her were the outer wraps - scanty, indeed, for such a day - of Lilama. On the left, as Pym swept at a glance the apartment, he saw the maid Ixza, reclining in a large chair; she, also, to all appearances, was asleep. Then he saw his wife. She crouched on the floor at the foot of the lounge, only her wealth of light golden hair at first visible. Stepping to her side, Pym saw her, as many times in the ducal gardens he had seen her drop to the ground in her girlish fashion, to rest. Her arms were intertwined upon the foot of the lounge, her head resting upon them; and there the tired, childlike young wife had gone to sleep - forever.

"How beautiful she was in death! The gentle hand that had never touched the person of another but in helpfulness - how fair, how pallid; the fond sweet eyes that knew no glance but that of love and kindness - they were almost hidden by the drooping lids; the tenderest, loveliest face the sunlight ever kissed, smiled upward at him as he gazed - his heart felt colder than was this dear form he dropped beside and clasped. But the lips - the ripe red lips - the rapturous, maidenly lips, the first touch of which had raised him forever from the coarse earth - the arch lips that had bewitched him with their own seductive smile, and could not shape themselves to harsher act than pouting - a fleeting pout, that captivated ere it vanished - he could not look at them in death - he could not.

"Sweet child of a weird land and a strange people! She was one of those whose spotless souls need not the purifying fire of a long earthly life. For Pym, now and later, the sorrow and the yearning void; for her, only an earlier advancement.

"Pym's mind was shocked; but behind the shock he felt the awful anguish of such a separation. Was this the end? Could it be the end? For him, truly that day his last hope for this life died. But hereafter? Surely this was not to be the end of all! A few more years of grovelling on the clay bosom of the cold, selfish earth, and then - only oblivion? No, no: he would not, he could not believe it.

"As Pym stood there, where many, many other men have stood, and millions yet will stand, did his soul rise into the heavenly atmosphere, or did it question God's decrees and sink to rise no more? This I cannot answer.

"After such a loss, oh, the weary weight of unutterable woe; the awful sense that hope is dead, whilst the mourner can only stand with streaming eyes and bleeding heart, forever chained to the ghastly corpse of every dear ambition, of every joy, and all that our universe of feeling builds on hope. But we should learn from such a loss a lesson, for the lesson if learned insures our own advancement: such losses are but the purposes of God unfolding for those we love and for ourselves an eternity of blissful harmony."

Thus Doctor Bainbridge closed; and, though his words were of death, and the thoughts which he expressed were as old as the human race, I was much affected by them. Young as was the speaker, his utterances conveyed to me the impression that he himself had in some way learned the lesson of which he spoke. For several moments we sat in silence; and then, though I knew that he would have a few more words to say, I thought it an appropriate time to thank him for his long, painstaking elaboration of the old sailor's disclosures, which, as I knew partly from my own personal knowledge, had been gained only by untiring perseverance and inexhaustible patience. I thanked him, and complimented him as I thought he deserved; and he was pleased, I plainly saw, with the few words of commendation which he knew came from my heart.

We sat, smoking our cigars and chatting on various topics, until it was almost the hour at which he usually said to me goodnight. Then he returned to the Peters' story, saying:

"It only remains for me properly to dispose of Pym and Peters. Peters knows no more - in fact, not as much - of Pym after he returned home, as do we. Poe, we know, in the note to his 'Narrative,' alludes to 'the late sudden and distressing death of Mr. Pym.' This is all we know, and even this fact, when I told it to Peters, was new to him; for Pym and Peters parted in the month of February, 1830, at the City of Montevideo, Uruguay; Peters, with an old sailor chum, whom he happened to meet in South America, shipping to Australia; and Pym, a few days later, starting for the United States.

"It had no doubt been the policy of the Hili-lites to prevent all strangers from returning to the outer world; but this policy was, it seems, not a firmly founded one, and many circumstances arose to modify and finally even to reverse it. They looked upon Pym almost as one of themselves. When he left them, it was with the intention of returning; and they exacted of him a promise to hide, even from Peters, the longitudes traversed during the entire journey from Hili-li until they should touch the land of some civilized people, or meet with a ship; to which promise Pym rigidly adhered. And though they were in other ways very kind to him, they would not allow him to take away a single grain of gold, of which nuggets were as plentiful in the fissures of the Olympian ranges as are pebbles in the beds of mountain streams; nor would they allow him to retain, of the many precious stones in his possession, even the ruby which Lilama had given him; and no amount of argument or pleading could move them to a different decision. The Hili-lites were anxious to get rid of Peters, which had much to do with their willingness to 'speed the parting guest.' It seems that Pym for months after the death of Lilama was in an extremely morbid state of mind. He spent most of his time with Masusaelili, who allowed him to see Lilama's apparition or wraith many times. The aged mystic explained to Pym the scientific *modus operandi* of the production, so that he was in no way deceived into thinking that he met Lilama in person; but we may presume that, as it is to each of us some gratification to look at a painting or a photograph of a departed friend, it must have been a still greater pleasure for Pym thus to have reproduced for him the living, moving form and features of his lost darling - reproduced or simulated in such a manner that he might see her, and touch her, and hear her voice - even though he was told that the image was only a likeness. During Pym's abstraction, Peters was left almost entirely to himself; and his worst qualities, long inactive (partly because there had not been opportunity for their display, and partly because of Pym's influence), now came prominently to the surface. He associated with the wildest characters on the neighboring islands, making them even wilder and more ungovernable than before his arrival. Finally, with revenge for an excuse, but in reality from sheer restlessness, he began to organize a raid on the outlying barbarians, more particularly, he still avers, because he wished 'to get even with old Too-wit' and his barbarian followers for having murdered his companions, as described in Pym's diary. This the Hili-lites thought was going too far; and as it was now October, the Council of State decided to allow Pym to depart for home, taking Peters with him.

"One bright December morning these two toys of fortune said good-by to their kind hosts, and started on their long and perilous journey. A strong and handsome though small sail-boat had been provided for them. A number of Hili-lite youths - among them some of the former exiles - were to accompany them past the great antarctic continent; and for this piloting party a larger boat had been built. After many days, the continent was passed; and Pym and Peters, alone, began their wearisome voyage across the great Antarctic Ocean. Fortunately, in January they encountered a large schooner, which six weeks later, in February, landed them at Montevideo. Peters says that Montevideo was at that time - 1830 - little more than a walled fortress. This scarcely harmonizes with the fact that it was then, as now, the capital of Uruguay; but Peters appears to know what he is talking about. As I have said, at this place Pym and Peters parted, never to meet again. The younger man started for his home, and found an early grave; the older man sought new adventures, and he, at the age of eighty, still lives to tell of their adventures had in a country strange beyond man's credulity to believe."

These were the last words spoken by Doctor Bainbridge on the subject of Peters' adventures. Two days later I said farewell to my American friends, the memory of whom has always been dear to me, and whom it has been my misfortune not again to meet. The day before my departure, I drove to Peters' home, and said to him good-by. I called on Doctor Bainbridge at his office; and Doctor Castleton I met on the street corner, where, from the window of my apartment in the Loomis House, I had first seen him. I hope that the later life of each of them has been a smooth one: I know that both were good men, and that one of them was a man of singular fascination.

As I took my leave of Doctor Castleton, and after he had spoken of the death of Lilama, he said:

"I trust, young man, that you are pleased with your discovery - I know that Bainbridge is;" and he accompanied the remark with a searching glance of those large black eyes, the meaning of which I could not then fathom, and the recollection of which has often puzzled me. Then he smiled, and said farewell.

Doctor Bainbridge, when I had said my last words to him, spoke thus:

"May you have a pleasant journey, and a loving welcome to your home. You will probably never return to America - or, even if you do, not to our little city. I wish I could think that some day we shall meet again, but we probably never shall. And yet," he continued, smilingly, "who knows! If not again in this life, or in this world, still in some new form, on some strange planet. It may be that on Venus the beautiful our hands shall once more clasp; or on some water-way of Mars the ruddy, as we pass in our gondolas, we may call a greeting to each other - or possibly to Poe, the bright unfortunate. I am sorry that you must leave us, and I wish you every happiness."

It was at the railroad station, to which his duties called him, that I said to Arthur good-by; and there, as the train pulled out, through the car-window I caught a glimpse of two moist eyes looking after the departing train.

And now, to the patient reader, I say farewell.

Choose from Thousands of 1stWorldLibrary Classics By

A. M. Barnard
Ada Leverson
Adolphus William Ward
Aesop
Agatha Christie
Alexander Aaronsohn
Alexander Kielland
Alexandre Dumas
Alfred Gatty
Alfred Ollivant
Alice Duer Miller
Alice Turner Curtis
Alice Dunbar
Ambrose Bierce
Amelia E. Barr
Amory H. Bradford
Andrew Lang
Andrew McFarland Davis
Andy Adams
Anna Sewell
Annie Besant
Annie Hamilton Donnell
Annie Payson Call
Annonaymous
Anton Chekhov
Arnold Bennett
Arthur Conan Doyle
Arthur M. Winfield
Arthur Ransome
Atticus
B.H. Baden-Powell
B. M. Bower
Baroness Emmuska Orczy
Baroness Orczy
Basil King
Bayard Taylor
Ben Macomber
Bertha Muzzy Bower
Bjornstjerne Bjornson
Booth Tarkington
Boyd Cable
Bram Stoker
C. Collodi
C. E. Orr
C. M. Ingleby
Carolyn Wells
Catherine Parr Traill
Charles A. Eastman
Charles Dickens

Charles Dudley Warner
Charles Farrar Browne
Charles Ives
Charles Kingsley
Charles Klein
Charles Amory Beach
Charles Hanson Towne
Charles Lathrop Pack
Charles Whibley
Charles Willing Beale
Charlotte M. Braeme
Charlotte M. Yonge
Charlotte Perkins Stetson
Clair W. Hayes
Clarence Day Jr.
Clarence E. Mulford
Clemence Housman
Confucius
Cornelis DeWitt Wilcox
Cyril Burleigh
D. H. Lawrence
Daniel Defoe
David Garnett
Dinah Craik
Don Carlos Janes
Donald Keyhoe
Dorothy Kilner
Dougan Clark
Douglas Fairbanks
E. Nesbit
E.P.Roe
E. Phillips Oppenheim
Earl Barnes
Edgar Rice Burroughs
Edith Van Dyne
Edith Wharton
Edward J. O'Biren
Edward S. Ellis
Edwin L. Arnold
Eleanor Atkins
Eliot Gregory
Elizabeth Gaskell
Elizabeth McCracken
Elizabeth Von Arnim
Ellem Key
Emerson Hough
Emilie F. Carlen
Emily Dickinson
Enid Bagnold

Enilor Macartney Lane
Erasmus W. Jones
Ernie Howard Pie
Ethel Turner
Ethel Watts Mumford
Eugenie Foa
Eugene Wood
Eustace Hale Ball
Evelyn Everett-green
Everard Cotes
F. H. Cheley
F. J. Cross
Federick Austin Ogg
Ferdinand Ossendowski
Francis Bacon
Francis Darwin
Frances Hodgson Burnett
Frances Parkinson Keyes
Frank Gee Patchin
Frank Harris
Frank Jewett Mather
Frank L. Packard
Frank V. Webster
Frederic Stewart Isham
Frederick Trevor Hill
Frederick Winslow Taylor
Friedrich Kerst
Friedrich Nietzsche
Fyodor Dostoyevsky
G.A. Henty
G.K. Chesterton
Gabrielle E. Jackson
Garrett P. Serviss
Gaston Leroux
George A. Warren
George Ade
Geroge Bernard Shaw
George Durston
George Ebers
George Eliot
George Gissing
George MacDonald
George Meredith
George Orwell
George Sylvester Viereck
George Tucker
George W. Cable
George Wharton James
Gertrude Atherton

Grace E. King
Grace Gallatin
Grant Allen
Guillermo A. Sherwell
Gulielma Zollinger
Gustav Flaubert
H. A. Cody
H. B. Irving
H.C. Bailey
H. G. Wells
H. H. Munro
H. Irving Hancock
H. Rider Haggard
H. W. C. Davis
Hamilton Wright Mabie
Hans Christian Andersen
Harold Avery
Harold McGrath
Harriet Beecher Stowe
Harry Houidini
Helent Hunt Jackson
Helen Nicolay
Hendrik Conscience
Hendy David Thoreau
Henri Barbusse
Henrik Ibsen
Henry Adams
Henry Ford
Henry Frost
Henry James
Henry Jones Ford
Henry Seton Merriman
Henry W Longfellow
Herbert A. Giles
Herbert N. Casson
Herman Hesse
Homer
Honore De Balzac
Horace Walpole
Horatio Alger Jr.
Howard Pyle
Howard R. Garis
Hugh Lofting
Hugh Walpole
Humphry Ward
Ian Maclaren
Inez Haynes Gillmore
Irving Bacheller
Israel Abrahams
Ivan Turgenev
J.G.Austin

J. Henri Fabre
J. M. Barrie
J. Macdonald Oxley
J. S. Fletcher
J. S. Knowles
J. Storer Clouston
Jack London
Jacob Abbott
James Allen
James Andrews
James Baldwin
James DeMille
James Joyce
James Lane Allen
James Lane Allen
James Oliver Curwood
James Oppenheim
James Otis
James R. Driscoll
Jane Austen
Janet Aldridge
Jens Peter Jacobsen
Jerome K. Jerome
John Burroughs
John Cournos
John F. Kennedy
John Gay
John Glasworthy
John Habberton
John Joy Bell
John Kendrick Bangs
John Milton
John Philip Sousa
Jonas Lauritz Idemil Lie
Jonathan Swift
Joseph A. Altsheler
Joseph Carey
Joseph Conrad
Joseph E. Badger Jr
Joseph Hergesheimer
Joseph Jacobs
Jules Vernes
Julian Hawthrone
Julie A Lippmann
Justin Huntly McCarthy
Kakuzo Okakura
Kenneth Grahame
Kenneth McGaffey
Kate Langley Bosher
Kate Langley Bosher
Katherine Cecil Thurston

Katherine Stokes
L. A. Abbot
L. T. Meade
L. Frank Baum
Latta Griswold
Laura Lee Hope
Laurence Housman
Lawrence Beasley
Leo Tolstoy
Leonid Andreyev
Lewis Carroll
Lewis Sperry Chafer
Lilian Bell
Lloyd Osbourne
Louis Hughes
Louis Tracy
Louisa May Alcott
Lucy Fitch Perkins
Lucy Maud Montgomery
Lydia Miller Middleton
Lyndon Orr
M. Corvus
M. H. Adams
Margaret E. Sangster
Margaret Vandercook
Margret Penrose
Maria Edgeworth
Maria Thompson Daviess
Mariano Azuela
Marion Polk Angellotti
Mark Overton
Mark Twain
Mary Austin
Mary Catherine Crowley
Mary Cole
Mary Hastings Bradley
Mary Roberts Rinehart
Mary Rowlandson
M. Wollstonecraft Shelley
Maud Lindsay
Max Beerbohm
Myra Kelly
Nathaniel Hawthrone
Nicolo Machiavelli
O. F. Walton
Oscar Wilde
Owen Johnson
P.G. Wodehouse
Paul and Mabel Thorne
Paul G. Tomlinson
Paul Severing

Percy Brebner
Peter B. Kyne
Plato
R. Derby Holmes
R. L. Stevenson
R. S. Ball
Rabindranath Tagore
Rahul Alvares
Ralph Bonehill
Ralph Henry Barbour
Ralph Victor
Ralph Waldo Emmerson
Rene Descartes
Rex Beach
Rex E. Beach
Richard Harding Davis
Richard Jefferies
Richard Le Gallienne
Robert Barr
Robert Frost
Robert Gordon Anderson
Robert L. Drake
Robert Lansing
Robert Lynd
Robert Michael Ballantyne
Robert W. Chambers
Rosa Nouchette Carey
Rudyard Kipling
Samuel B. Allison

Samuel Hopkins Adams
Sarah Bernhardt
Sarah C. Hallowell
Selma Lagerlof
Sherwood Anderson
Sigmund Freud
Standish O'Grady
Stanley Weyman
Stella Benson
Stephen Crane
Stewart Edward White
Stijn Streuvels
Swami Abhedananda
Swami Parmananda
T. S. Ackland
T. S. Arthur
The Princess Der Ling
Thomas A. Janvier
Thomas A Kempis
Thomas Anderton
Thomas Bailey Aldrich
Thomas Bulfinch
Thomas De Quincey
Thomas H. Huxley
Thomas Hardy
Thomas More
Thornton W. Burgess
U. S. Grant
Valentine Williams

Various Authors
Vaughan Kester
Victor Appleton
Virginia Woolf
Walter Camp
Walter Scott
Washington Irving
Wilbur Lawton
Wilkie Collins
Willa Cather
Willard F. Baker
William Dean Howells
William le Queux
W. Makepeace Thackeray
William W. Walter
Winston Churchill
Yei Theodora Ozaki
Yogi Ramacharaka
Young E. Allison
Zane Grey

www.ingramcontent.com/pod-product-compliance
Lightning Source LLC
Chambersburg PA
CBHW031342170626
46807CB00002B/796